Praise for *Gabriel*

A meticulously-written, thought-provoking, massively-relevant, deeply-moving tale! "The King of Hearts" should be required reading at the middle-school level and above. The advanced vocabulary in the latter pages is a challenge but easily surmounted. Bravo!

—Paul Cooper, former president of the
Southfield, Michigan Board of Education

The aptness of the name Gabriel is not lost on the reader. The original Gabriel was an archangel who served as God's messenger and was the only archangel sometimes represented as a woman. If you are of a religious or historical bent, you will like that echo. If you are purely secular, it is enough to know that Gabriel brings us messages from the hidden parts of ourselves that we try to overlook as we chase after status.

—Dori Hale, author of *Disorientation and the Weather*

Read this book if you are open to receiving laser-sharp insights from a prepubescent squirrel. Read it if you are struggling to find your own way in an oft-unkind world. Read it if you much prefer acorns over pine nuts.

—Barry Cook, former vice president, NBC

As the Buddha lay dying, he uttered his final piece of advice to his mourning students: "Be a lamp unto yourself; work out your own awakening with diligence." The idea is that we are all utterly complete, lacking nothing, but are ignorant about how this is so. Yet at the same time, we all need some help finding that wisdom, needing spiritual mentors who have themselves found their way and can nudge the rest of us towards our own awakening. This, in a nutshell, is the essence of Tom Fitzgerald's fable *Gabriel: King of Hearts*. It is a moving, wise, and beautifully written retelling of the timeless spiritual lesson finding our own inner wisdom, and how one of our greatest gifts to ourselves and our world is to share this wisdom with all who seek it. By turns funny, heart-breaking, thought-provoking and tender, this is a book that will inspire you on your journey.

—Ban Nyo Sho Shin, Zen student

A Fable for Adults and Near-Adults

GABRIEL

King of Hearts

TOM FITZGERALD

Author of Poor Richard's Lament

KINGSLEY BOOKS

North Kingstown, Rhode Island

Cover art by Steve Lindsay

Composed in Whitman at Hobblebush Design
(www.hobblebush.com)

First Kingsley Books edition published January 2019

Printed in the United States of America

ISBN: 978-1-7325479-2-6

KINGSLEY BOOKS

215 Buena Vista Drive
North Kingstown, RI 02852-6307
www.kingsley-books.com

I went to the woods because I wished to live deliberately, to front only the essential facts of life, and see if I could not learn what it had to teach, and not, when I came to die, discover that I had not lived.

—HENRY DAVID THOREAU
Walden, 1854

The truth of us
is the tooth of us

One

"Gabriel! Time to get up, honey!"

He was still asleep.

"Hey, up there; you awake?"

He was dreaming.

"Gabriel, you're going to be late for the bus! C'mon—shake a leg!"

Which one?

"Hey, up there! Answer me!"

He was far too sick to move.

"Gabriel! I don't have time for this! You're going to make me late for work!"

He was at death's holeway.

Hearing the door open, Gabriel pressed his eyes shut and held his breath.

An itch behind his left ear suddenly flared into easily the worst itch he'd ever had in his entire life. He couldn't scratch it, though, without bagging himself. One can't be both breathing his last breath and scratching an itch.

A gentle touch on his shoulder triggered a rush of relief.

Cracking his eyes open, Gabriel could see his mother looming over him, paws on hips. He rolled over onto his other side.

"Yeah, yeah."

"Why didn't you answer me?"

"I was asleep."

"Yeah, and my name is Cassandra Coconut. If I'm late for work one

A creative mind is the quill
pen of a rebellious spirit.

more time because of you missing your bus, buster, I'm going to lose my job. Then where would we be?"

"You don't even like your job. You hate it."

"Oh, so we can all do in this life just what we want to do? Is that it?"

"Why not?"

The door slammed, shaking, it seemed, the entire tree.

Gabriel savored a moment of triumph, but then, as in the case of a cloud passing over the sun, the full glare of reality soon returned. All he had really accomplished, he realized, was to hurt his mother's feelings yet again, after having just promised himself, yet again, that he would never cause either his mother or his stepfather any more grief. He would do whatever it took to make himself worthy of their smiles.

Gabriel felt a lump form in his throat as he recalled the incident, two Sundays ago, that had precipitated his latest vow of good behavior—

~

The Reverend Willow had called all the pups up to the front of the church for Story Time, and read them the Story of the First Dawn from the Book of Sacred Scratchings, and had then asked if anyone had a question.

For Gabriel, an unrequited curiosity was like an itch he could not reach with one of his own claws and so required someone's assistance. Only rarely, however, did he ever seek such assistance directly from an adult, except Master Learned. Even when adults invited questions, Gabriel had learned, often what they really wanted was the silence that was the flip side of obedience. This was especially true, he had discovered, in regard to the three R's: Religion, Reproduction, and Remarriage.

Unable on this occasion to keep silent concerning an "itch" that had been driving him nuts for several moons now, Gabriel raised a paw.

"Yes, my son," the Reverend Willow had said, holding a microphone so close to Gabriel's nose he had nearly touched it.

Although Gabriel had spoken in a normal voice, it had seemed to come out much louder: "Could the Great Rodent create a critter even more powerful than He?"

The Reverend's reaction had been swift and harsh. "Sacrilege!" he had barked. "Blasphemy! Be gone from this sacred tree, ye minion of the Dark One! Away with thee!"

In death, the great equalizer
is the casket; in life,
the commode.

~

The lump in Gabriel's throat began to burn. Tears welled.

He had not meant to be disrespectful. He had meant only to take advantage of an unexpected opportunity to satisfy an "itch" he had not been able to satisfy on his own since scratching in his journal, several moons ago now, a great curiosity: In order for the Great Rodent to be all-powerful, he had scratched, it would seem He would need to be able to create something even more powerful than Himself. If He could not, then how could He be all-powerful? There would be at least one thing He could not do. However, if He <u>could</u> create something even more powerful than Himself, and did, then He would no longer be all-powerful. What He had created would be. Help!

What he should have done, of course, was just keep his mouth shut, instead of thoughtlessly causing his parents likely the most grief they had ever known in all their seasons—

"We'll never be able to live this down," his stepfather had screeched. "Never."

"Nothing will ever be the same," his mother had wept. "Nothing."

Wiping the wet from his furry cheeks, Gabriel tightened the ball he was squeezed into, and closed his eyes—

~

As he hobbled back into the game, the crowd erupted into a thunderous roar, the likes of which Gabriel had never heard in all his seasons.

His injury would have kept any other player in the entire league on the sidelines for the rest of the season. He had been so badly injured, in fact, that he had had to be carried off the field on a stretcher. One of the players on the opposing team had deliberately hit him low, from behind.

His team was six points behind and there were only 30 seconds left on the clock. "You sure you can go in there?" the coach had asked. "I can do it, Coach" Gabriel had replied, wiping blood from his mouth. "Whatever it takes." Tears had flooded into the coach's eyes. Gabriel had never seen tears in the coach's eyes before.

As he stood waiting for his quarterback to bark out the signals, Gabriel could hear a hundred thousand voices chanting his name, over and over: "Gab-ri-el! Gab-ri-el! Gab-ri-el!"

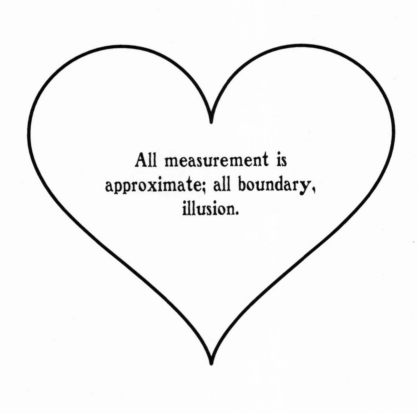

All measurement is
approximate; all boundary,
illusion.

"Nut one, nut two"—

The quarterback faded backward and pitched the pawnut to Gabriel. Tucking the pawnut firmly against his breast, Gabriel exploded into motion. As he scurried to his right, a huge, mean-looking tackle lunged for him, but Gabriel was easily able to elude a desperate grasp, despite the excruciating pain in his injured leg. Then another defender lunged at him, and another, and another.

"Gab-ri-el! Gab-ri-el!" the crowd chanted as Gabriel scurried and scampered, darted and dodged his way through the best defensive line in the entire league.

Suddenly he was in the clear!

No, there was still one defender between him and the goal line—the same player who had deliberately injured him earlier! He was coming directly at him, showing Gabriel a look that said he was going to hurt him again. He was going to make him look foolish in front of all these squirrels. He was going to make everybody laugh at him.

Not this time! Gabriel vowed to himself. This time, it was going to be the other way around!

Narrowing his eyes, Gabriel ran directly toward the onrushing defender.

Only a few tail lengths separated them—

Only a few paws—

~

"Gabriel!"

Gabriel bolted upright.

"Get out of that bed!"

Gabriel tore the covers off himself and sprang from his bed.

His stepfather pointed a sharp claw between his eyes. "And don't you ever talk to your mother that way again. You hear me?"

Gabriel nodded, feeling his stomach squeeze itself into as small a presence as possible, like a doomed mole cringing against a rock.

The look on his stepfather's face held more than anger. It was a look Gabriel had been seeing on his stepfather's face since the very day he had married his mother. It was a look that seemed to say: "I don't like you, Gabriel. In fact, I can't stand having you around. You're an embarrassment, and you're not mine; you're somebody else's little twit. I wish you'd

Hope is the stirrup we use
to climb into the saddle of
each new day.

go away and never come back." It was a look Gabriel had never once seen his stepfather direct toward anyone else, not even Cherice, even when she was being her brattiest, which was most of the time.

"I don't know what's gotten into you lately, buster," his stepfather scolded, "but it's going to have to stop, starting right now. You hear me?"

Gabriel nodded.

His stepfather slammed the door, rattling the entire tree.

Gabriel stood trembling. He couldn't stop. Finally, he sat down on the edge of his bed and hung his head. Tears rolled down his furry cheeks.

If he had tried just a little harder to win a place on the pawnut team, even if he had only made it onto the third string, at least his stepfather would have had one reason to be proud of him.

Gabriel stared at the floor, unable to do anything else. Finally, fearing a return visit from his stepfather, he put his thick, bottle-bottom glasses on and started to get dressed.

By the time he got to the kitchen, his stepfather had already left the tree for the butternut factory where he was in charge of the shucking department. It was early autumn, the time of the year when all the nut factories were operating at full capacity, which meant his stepfather would not return to the tree until well into the evening.

Good!

Gabriel's mother was hurrying to leave for work. As Gabriel sat staring at a bowlful of boiled nutmeal, his mother gathered her tote and her pocketbook and stood in front of the main holeway. Looking at Gabriel sternly, she warned him not to miss his bus, or else. The look on her face carried the usual freight of anger and fear. The anger was because of him, Gabriel knew; the fear, because of Mr. Larch, her boss, who did not like her to be late.

Gabriel's sister Cherice had already finished her breakfast and returned to her room to finish preening for school. Cherice was always preening, it seemed to Gabriel—devoting almost every waking moment to doing whatever it took to catch the attention of the letes at her school. If he were to be so reckless as to point this out to her, however, he well knew, she would call him a "genderist low-life scat-head" and proceed to scratch him bald, head to tail, as she had nearly succeeded in doing on more than one occasion, for much-lesser offenses.

Humility is the last lesson
learned, the first forgot.

Cherice was two years older and attended a different school. Hers was within walking distance; Gabriel had to take a bus to his.

Cherice entered the kitchen carrying her backpack and looking well preened. After a quick glance in her direction, Gabriel resumed staring down at his boiled nutmeal, which he had barely touched. It had grown cold and soggy because of his having taken so long to get himself out of bed.

Gabriel hated cold, soggy nutmeal.

"Don't forget to lock the holeway," Cherice admonished as she breezed past him.

Gabriel wrinkled his nose to a strong whiff of the flower-scent Cherice was wearing about nine splashes too much of.

"Mind your own business," he snapped.

"You're a scathead, Gabriel Maplewood," Cherice said, just before crawling out the holeway.

"So are you," Gabriel screeched.

After Cherice had gone, Gabriel dumped his boiled nutmeal into the garbage and went into the bathroom to brush his incisors. He took his time brushing so he wouldn't have to spend any more time at the bus stop than was absolutely unavoidable. Finally finished, he collected his school books and his lunch and the astronomy book he had checked out of the grove library on Saturday and putting these into his backpack, except for the astronomy book, which was too large, left the tree.

He deliberately left the holeway door unlocked.

It was Gabriel's favorite kind of morning. The maples were beginning to turn crimson and orange, and the aspens, already brightly yellow, seemed to combust in the early-morning sunshine. The air was cool in that snuggy sort of way that is peculiar to autumn, and the undergrowth, damp from a gentle, overnight rain, and still green, seemed particularly lush. It was not the kind of day, Gabriel said to himself, as he trudged toward the bus stop, that he should have to waste sitting in a tree full of squirrels who didn't seem to care about anything other than who was wearing what kind of sneaker or who was pulling whose tail.

Suddenly a deliciously happy thought popped into Gabriel's head, like a big wide grin on an invisible face. He could just turn around, right then and there, before anybody at the bus stop had a chance to see him, and scurry back to his tree to get his camera. He could spend the

Ignorance is the worst of evils
for it is the witch's brew of
all others.

whole rest of the day in the forest by himself, taking pictures, reading his astronomy book, and scratching thoughts into his journal—and just basking in the friendly autumn sun.

No one would even know. At school, they would think he was out sick for the day. Nobody else would even notice, much less give a care.

Gabriel waited for the big wide grin hovering in his mind to order him to turn around. Instead, it grew dimmer, and dimmer, until poof! it was gone.

You pigeon-twit! Gabriel screeched at himself. Bammer and Chopper were right! You're a complete and utter wimp! A sissified, yellow-bellied pigeon-twit! Only squirrels like Bammer and Chopper had the grease to do such dangerous things as skip school.

As Gabriel turned a corner, he could see Bammer and Chopper waiting at the bus stop with the usual group of pups.

"Hey, here comes Einey Hiney," Chopper screeched, noticing Gabriel approaching.

Gabriel prayed for the bus to arrive on time—Please!—even though he knew his plea would fall on deaf ears because of his recent violation of the fifth Indelible Don't: "Bring not shame unto your mother or your father."

"Desperation makes beggars of us all," Gabriel had once written in his journal.

Please!

Bammer approached Gabriel showing a look that made Gabriel's stomach begin to queaze and quiver. It was similar to the look Gabriel was always seeing on his stepfather's face.

"Whataya got there, Einey?" Bammer snatched the astronomy book out of Gabriel's paws. "Get a load of this," he barked, loud enough for everyone at the bus stop to hear: "Everything You Ever Wanted to Know about Being a Pigeon-Twit but Were Too Bleepin' Scared to Ask."

Everyone at the bus stop howled.

Gabriel pictured himself grabbing Bammer by the neck and pushing his face into a mud puddle. But, of course, he would never do anything of the kind.

Bammer began to paw through Gabriel's book with deliberate carelessness, injuring several pages.

Gabriel flinched with each excruciating sound of tearing paper, until

A single rose is an expression
of love; a dozen, an
admission of guilt.

finally he could bear the agony no longer. "Please," he pleaded, "give it back. You're hurting it."

Bammer ripped out part of a page. "Oh gee gosh, you're right. I think I just heard the poor thing scream. Did ya hear it?"

Gabriel struggled to hold back tears.

Bammer slowly ripped out most of another page. "Did ya hear that one?"

Tears flooded into Gabriel's eyes. "Yes, yes," he screeched, nodding.

Bammer jammed the ripped-out pages back into the book and handed the book to Gabriel. "Kiss it better," Bammer demanded. As Gabriel reached for the book, Bammer let go of it and jumped backward. The book landed in a mud puddle and splashed muddy water over Gabriel's hind legs.

Bammer and Chopper, bursting into screeches of laughter, were joined by the other squirrels at the bus stop.

Gabriel pawed his book out of the muddy water and wiping it off as best he could with his bushy tail, held the book against his breast.

Standing off by himself then, his face uplifted toward the sun, Gabriel closed his eyes and pictured himself stretched out on a high limb deep in the forest. He could feel his eyes become heavier in the healing warmth—his muscles become supple and relaxed—his soul become like a morning mist hanging over a tranquil pond—

Gabriel popped his eyes open to a jarring screech.

The bus had arrived.

Nature loathes
a straight line.

Two

Gabriel had been secretly reading from his astronomy book since finishing the last of the three birdfeeder problems that Master Learned had assigned to the class. Gabriel was holding the astronomy book open in a V on his lap. He had left his birdfeeder textbook open on his desk to make Master Learned think he was still working on the problems.

The chapter Gabriel had been reading, re-reading actually, was titled The Big Thunder. It was about that awesome burst of spontaneous creation billions of cycles ago that had resulted in the Great Forest and all its wonders

It made him dizzy with awe every time he read it.

He looked up at the wall clock.

The big paw and little paw showed 11:54.

Only one tick to go!

Any longer and he would start gnawing the top of his desk!

Hunger was one of the few forces in the universe that could pull Gabriel away from the subject dearest to his heart. Gabriel loved to read about things that made his brain feel as if it had been in a wrestling match with an angel.

Slipping his astronomy book inside his desk, Gabriel began to think his stomach had gotten so desperate that one end of it had begun to gnaw the other end. Next time, he told himself, he would eat his breakfast no matter how cold and soggy it was.

As his stepfather was always telling him, he was his own worst enemy!

The big paw on the wall clock snapped forward and a clamorous bell

Most of what glitters needs
constantly to be re-plated.

rang, triggering a commotion of pups putting away books and getting out lunch bags.

"Okay, class," Master Learned said, "you may"—

Before Master Learned could finish, Gabriel had jumped from his seat and, joining the rush toward the holeway, had managed to get in line at about the same place he usually did, about two-thirds the way to the rear. Chopper and Bammer were at the very front. The other letes were queued just behind them, roughly in order of their 'leteness.' Nobody ever challenged the letes' right to be first in line, not even Master Learned.

When the last chattery pup had quieted down, Master Learned led the way through the holeway and down the school tree to the lunch den.

As he usually did, Gabriel sat down at a table with several 'middle-tons.' Feeling hungry enough to eat chokeberries, he was about to chomp into a grainy slice of pinenut bread when a screech from Christopher stopped him. "Don't nobody chomp yet!" Christopher screeched.

Christopher was holding a pawnut card and looking, Gabriel thought, very pleased with himself. "Okay, guys," Christopher said, "now that I have your attention, what am I offered?"

"Who is it?" Tommy Uptree asked. Tommy was Christopher's biggest rival for having the best pawnut card collection of anyone in the entire school.

"Scurry McMurray," Christopher said. "When he was Rookie of The Year!"

"Fake! Fake!" Tommy screeched. "Nobody's got those but them rich collectors who live at the very top of big red oaks."

"Oh, yeah," Christopher said, looking even more pleased with himself. "Well, I got this one from my dad, who got it from one of the vice presidents at his company, who got it directly from Scurry McMurray himself!"

"Let me see that," Larry Littlepine demanded, grabbing the card out of Christopher's paw. Larry examined the signature closely. "Wow, that's real ink!"

Christopher grabbed his card back from Larry.

"I'll give you two wildberry nutcakes," Larry said.

"I'll give you a whole bag of honey-dipped sunflower seeds," Tommy Uptree said.

Power is rarely offered; you
must at least put in a request.

Gabriel glanced over at the table where Bammer and Chopper were sitting with several of the other letes—

Gabriel pictured himself approaching his two biggest tormentors.

"This is for you," Gabriel said, pawing the Rookie of the Year card toward Chopper.

Chopper frowned, but then lit up like an April dawn.

"Wow! Scurry McMurray! Wow! Rookie of the Year! Gee, thanks, Gabriel—'ol buddy. Hey, how about you being on my team today at recess?"

Catching himself smiling, Gabriel glanced around the table to see if anyone had noticed.

"Anyone else?" Christopher asked.

Gabriel stared down at his lunch. Having not eaten any breakfast, he was hungry enough to eat raw pinenuts—a whole treeful!

"Going—going—"

"I'll give you my whole lunch," Gabriel blurted.

"Your whole lunch?" Christopher asked. "The whole thing?"

Gabriel nodded.

"Whataya got?"

Gabriel showed Christopher his two slices of dry, grainy pinenut bread and his tub of milkweed yogurt.

Christopher stared at Gabriel's offerings without saying a word. No one said a word. It was as if everyone at the table had been struck dumb by the accidental incantations of a sorcerer apprentice. Then Christopher's face took on a look reminiscent of the time Master Learned had asked him to recite the full text of the Bill of Responsibilities from memory.

Gabriel, desperate for a place to hide, began to curse himself for having lacked the courage to play hooky.

"Don't you have any wildberry cakes or nutmeat pies or anything?" Christopher finally asked.

Gabriel shook his head.

Christopher gave a shrug, then turned to Alan Autumn-Oak. "Sold! for two wild blueberry sugar tarts."

Gabriel watched Alan Autumn-Oak, the fattest pup in the entire school, give Christopher two large wild blueberry sugar tarts and accept the Scurry McMurray Rookie of the Year card as if it were a trophy won in mortal combat.

The quality of a relationship
is the quality of the two
people in it.

Gabriel was tempted to say something nasty to Alan—something like, "Hey, Thunder Butt, careful you don't choke to death trying to eat both those tarts at once." But, of course, he said nothing of the kind. Only pups like Bammer and Chopper had the courage to say really nasty things to squirrels bigger than they were.

Gabriel ate his lunch in silence and then went outside with the other pups for recess. A few of the middleton boys, and most of the middleton girls, went to the playground area to slide and swing, while the grungies slipped out of sight to do all those unhealthy things that adult squirrels were always warning pups not to do. The royals arranged themselves on low-lying limbs like ornaments, and preened.

Gabriel followed the letes and most of the middletons to the pawnut field, where Bammer and Chopper took it upon themselves, as they always did, to choose up sides. They chose up the other letes first, selecting them more or less in the same order they lined up for lunch; then they chose up the middletons.

As Bammer and Chopper took turns, Gabriel found himself hoping, as always, that he would not be the very last pup to be chosen. Why don't you choose Alan Autumn-Oak last? he muttered to himself. He's so fat he can hardly move. Can't you guys see I'm better than he is?

Finally there were only two pups left to be chosen.

Gabriel held his breath.

"Oakie," Bammer said.

Gabriel felt a familiar heaviness descend upon him, as when he first awakened on a Monday morning.

"Einey," Chopper said, in a tone of voice that seemed to Gabriel to say, "Well, if I've got to choose you, you little pigeon-twit, I guess I've got to, but I sure don't wanna."

Watching Alan Autumn-Oak waddle off with his teammates, Gabriel narrowed his eyes to slits and vowed that this would be absolutely the last time he'd ever be chosen dead last—ever again. He was going to get himself so wide open down field that Chopper would simply have no choice but to throw him the pawnut—for a sure touchdown.

As usual, Chopper assigned all the glory positions to his fellow letes, all the dirty-work positions to the middletons, and no position at all to Gabriel. Anticipating this deliberate slight, Gabriel did what he always did; he assigned himself a position, as extra-wide receiver.

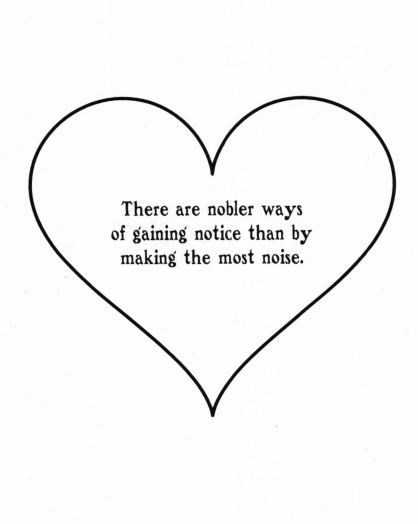

There are nobler ways
of gaining notice than by
making the most noise.

Five times Gabriel managed to get himself completely open, twice while standing alone in the end zone, but not once did Chopper even look his way.

With the score tied, and recess nearly over, Chopper called one last play in the huddle. He used a stick to draw a sketch of the routes he wanted each of his receivers to run. Gabriel drew a route for himself inside his head, picturing just where he would most likely be open. Then he lined up on the line of scrimmage, near where Scooter Sweetgum, the right end, was crouched, and waited for Chopper to bark the correct signal.

When he heard Chopper bark "nut two," Gabriel sprang into motion. He sprinted forward, faked left, scurried right, twirled, scampered left, and found himself all alone near the left sideline of the field. Not a single defender was within fifteen tails of him.

Gabriel began to wave his arms to get Chopper's attention, but Chopper, as usual, was preoccupied with finding one of his buddies to throw to. Then two of the pass rushers on Bammer's team got past their blockers and began to close in on Chopper. For a moment longer, Chopper continued to try to find one of his buddies open down field, but then, after just barely eluding a lunge by Alan Autumn-Oak, Chopper tucked the pawnut against his breast and scurried to his right, apparently deciding to make a desperate run for the goal line.

There was no chance of his team winning now, Gabriel knew, because Chopper, as good a scurrier as he was, had no chance of making it all the way to the goal line without getting tagged. Bammer, the fastest lete in the whole school, would get him.

If only you had thrown it to me, Gabriel said to himself, we might have won.

Just before reaching the line of scrimmage, Chopper suddenly cocked his arm, sidewise, and rifled the pawnut directly toward Gabriel!

Gabriel was so stunned by what could not possibly be happening that, by the time he was able to convince himself it actually was happening, it was too late to react. The bullet-like pawnut bounced off his chest, nearly knocking him over.

"You jerk!" he heard Bubba Jay screech.

"You stupid crow!" he heard Chopper screech.

"You banana head!" he heard Chucky Cheeks screech.

To pursue the sweet is to
risk the sour.

"Nice catch," Bammer barked, grinning. "It's always nice to have you playing on the other team."

All the squirrels on Bammer's team began to howl.

Gabriel tried to summon the words that would make them all understand what had happened. He had merely frozen for a moment, because he had not been expecting a pass, because no one had ever thrown him a pass before. Maybe if Chopper had called his name in the huddle—maybe if Chopper had thrown him a pass at least once previously—

But the words would not come.

"Next time, do us all a big favor and go play with the girls," Chopper said. "Where you belong."

With tears pushing their way into his eyes, Gabriel turned away and scurried off the field.

"Good riddance, you little pigeon-twit," he heard Chopper screech after him.

Closing his eyes, Gabriel saw himself standing at the edge of Kieff's Cliff, eyes closed, arms outstretched—and found himself on the ground, flat on his back. He had run smack into a tree. Behind him, the letes were screeching hard enough to be heard by every predator in the forest. Gabriel hoped, anyway.

Springing onto the offending tree, Gabriel scurried to the far side, and then climbed up and up and up until he was higher even than Chopper or Bammer dared go.

Swaying in the chill breeze, he closed his eyes, and bowed his head. The back of his throat began to sting as if from unripened winterberries. When the bell rang, signaling the end of recess, Gabriel pretended he didn't hear it.

He was just having another bad dream.

When he was ready, he would wake up—not before.

When he did wake up, everything would be the way it was before his real father left the tree late one night without even saying good-bye.

Own not, owe not.

Three

When Gabriel arrived home from school, his parents were still at work and his sister was still at school. At this time of year, Cherice always stayed after school for cheerleading practice.

Gabriel hated coming home to an empty tree. He hated it even more than opening the refrigerator to find nothing inside except a few shriveled-up hazelnuts and a half-empty tub of milkweed yoghurt. He especially hated it when he needed someone to read his face the moment he came through the holeway and gently coax him into talking about what was wrong.

Standing in the kitchen, Gabriel glanced up at the wall clock. The paws read 3:47. Cherice would be arriving home any minute.

Gabriel thought about telling Cherice what had happened at recess, but decided against it. Cherice would just shake her head and say something like, "So why didn't you just catch the pass? That's what you wanted, isn't it?"

Some squirrels asked questions as a way of trying to make things better; others, as a way of trying to make things worse. Cherice was an absolute master at the latter.

Gabriel checked the contents of each of the snack jars his mother kept on the counter near the refrigerator, but none of the usual fare appealed to him. He frowned at the butternut flakes, wrinkled his nose at the acorn meal, and yukked at the sunflower hearts. Then a picture popped into his head of the wild blueberry sugar tarts that Alan Autumn-Oak had traded for Christopher's Scurry McMurray pawnut card, which, Gabriel

To get what we need, we
must let go of what we want.

had since decided, was a fake. What he really wanted, Gabriel realized, were the kinds of treats all the other pups got to snack on when they arrived home from school.

Gabriel was suddenly visited by a thought darker even than the darkest dark chocolate.

Why not? He deserved it!

Standing on a chair pulled from the kitchen table, Gabriel lifted a canister from the cupboard above the refrigerator, and hurrying the canister to the table, clawed off the lid. His heart sank. There were only four chocolate-covered walnuts left. If he took even one, it would be missed the next time his mother got treats out to celebrate the next special occasion—probably when Cherice got elected captain of her cheerleading squad, as she darn well knew she was going to be, despite all her phony protestations to the contrary. Gabriel liked that word—protestations.

About to return the canister to the shelf over the refrigerator, Gabriel was visited by a thought even darker than the previous one.

Why not? He deserved it!

Ripping the lid off the canister, Gabriel pawed out two of the remaining four chocolate-covered walnuts, and a third, leaving one.

If his mother had been home, Gabriel assured himself, he wouldn't have been able to take even one. So it was really all her fault that there wouldn't be enough treats to go around when the big news came that Cherice had been elected captain of her stupid cheering squad.

Anything left unguarded was fair game. Wasn't that the way the world really worked?

Sitting down in the same chair he had used as a stepstool, Gabriel began to nibble at one of the chocolate-covered walnuts. As usual, he nibbled it in such a way as to leave most of the chocolate coating intact, to be relished last.

Finished with the first walnut, Gabriel began to nibble at the second, but had managed to eat only about halfway through the meat when he heard the sound of sharp claws on the trunk outside. Jumping up from his chair, Gabriel stuffed the remainder of the half-eaten walnut into one of his pockets, the third walnut in another pocket, then quickly used the chair to put the canister back in the cupboard over the refrigerator.

"Hi!" Cherice said, as she crawled through the main holeway, not half a second after Gabriel had returned the chair to the table.

Memory is more novelist
than librarian.

"How 'bout a game of Power Paw?" Gabriel asked.

Cherice sighed. "Oh, Gabriel, gimme a break, will ya. I just got home." Cherice dropped her backpack heavily on the table. "What's for snacks?"

"Frosted mole pellets."

Cherice wrinkled her nose. "Aren't you ever going to grow up, Gabriel Maplewood?"

"Why should I? It hasn't exactly done you any good."

Cherice rolled her eyes and glanced at the table where Gabriel had just been sitting. "What'd you have?"

"How 'bout just one game?" Gabriel said.

Cherice eyed the row of canisters on the counter next to the refrigerator, and frowned toward Gabriel. "No, I do not want to play any of your silly computer games," she snapped.

"What's the matter," Gabriel said, "afraid little brother might beat big sister?"

Cherice pulled a sunflower heart from one of the canisters on the counter. "Look, I just don't feel like playing right now, OK? Besides, I told Sally I'd call her."

"Pigeon-twit."

Cherice narrowed her eyes. "Okay, buster," she snapped, "you asked for it. But just one game and that's it."

Gabriel scurried into the family room, powered up the game box, and brought up the Power Paw flash screen. Cherice knelt down beside him.

"You ready?" Gabriel asked, pushing one of the control sticks toward his sister.

Cherice quickly finished her sunflower heart. "Ready," she said, brushing her paws together.

Narrowing his eyes, Gabriel moved the cursor onto the start icon and clicked the left mole button. Not only was he going to beat his dumb sister; he was going to absolutely humiliate her. He was going to crush her 30 to nothing! No, 50 to nothing! No, 70 to nothing! And then he was going to take a chocolate-covered walnut out of his pocket and start nibbling it right in front of her!

On the very first play, Gabriel's quarterback passed the electronic pawnut right into the paws of one of Cherice's defensive players. Before Gabriel could even shift into defense, Cherice had easily maneuvered her interceptor into the end zone for a touchdown.

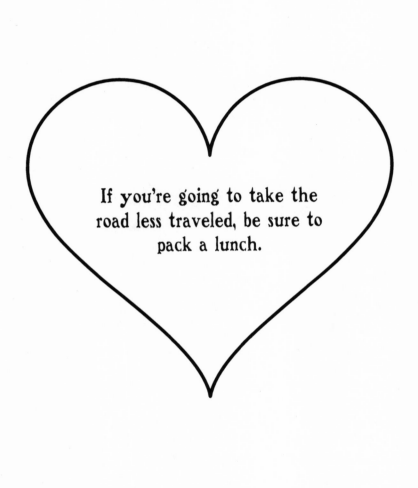

If you're going to take the
road less traveled, be sure to
pack a lunch.

"Yahoo!" Cherice screeched.

Gabriel exploded. He screeched all the obscenities he had ever heard on the After Hours channel; he pounded his control stick several times on the floor; he jumped up and kicked the game box, sending it crashing to the floor.

The screen flashed brilliantly, then went dark.

Cherice jumped back in horror. "You broke it!" she screeched. "You broke it!"

"Good!" Gabriel screeched back, giving the monitor another sharp kick.

"Stop it!" Cherice screeched. "Dad's gonna kill you!"

Gabriel stared hard at the confusion of fear and disgust on Cherice's face. "Good!" he screeched. "That's what he's always wanted to do anyway."

Tears flooding into his eyes, Gabriel bounded into the kitchen and using Cherice's backpack as a sledgehammer smashed one and a half chocolate-covered walnuts on top of the kitchen table. He then bounded through the main holeway.

~

When finally Gabriel returned home, cold and hungry, his stepfather was even angrier, and scarier, than when Gabriel had asked the Reverend Willow the forbidden question about the Great Rodent. His mother was angry, too, but she was more upset over having found chocolate and nut crumbs on the kitchen table, and three chocolate-covered walnuts missing from the treats canister, than she was about the broken game box. "That was a selfish, selfish thing to do, Gabriel Maplewood," his mother screeched. "Shame on you."

After telling Gabriel he would have to pay for a new game box by selling his camera, Gabriel's stepfather sent him to his room for the night—no supper, no nothing.

Laying on his bed now, his stomach churning with hunger, Gabriel turned his head until he could read the clock on his nightstand. The paws read 10:06.

If his mother was going to sneak him something to eat, she would have done it by now.

Closing his eyes, Gabriel pictured how his mother and stepfather would look the moment they learned that their only son had just been

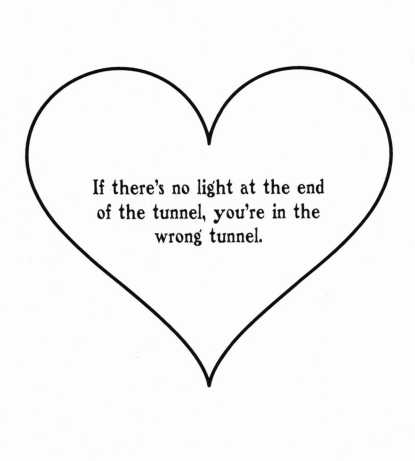

If there's no light at the end
of the tunnel, you're in the
wrong tunnel.

found in a broken heap at the bottom of Kieff's Cliff with his camera, smashed to bits, at his side. He pictured how they would react when the note found in his chocolate-stained pants pocket was read out loud to them: "I'm sorry I was so much trouble. It won't happen again."

A tear rolled down Gabriel's cheek.

He wondered if Chopper and Bammer would feel guilty for having treated him so badly.

He couldn't imagine it. Squirrels like Bammer and Chopper never seemed to feel guilty about anything.

The sound of his stepfather's voice from below interrupted Gabriel's thoughts. "Go! Go! Go!" he heard his stepfather screech.

"Touchdown! Woohoo!"

Gabriel's stepfather was down in the family room watching Thursday Night Pawnut. The North Country Pines, Scurry McMurray's team, was playing the Faraway Oaks.

"Scurry McMurray is absolutely the greatest!" Gabriel heard his stepfather screech. "I've never seen anyone scurry the way that squirrel can."

~

It was just after the big game. His uniform was stained and torn. His body was bruised and bloodied. He was standing beside his stepfather, towering over him. No, it was his real father. No, it was his stepfather.

His real father was dead.

Several TV cameras were aimed at him. One of those motor-mouth ex-player commentators was asking him the usual dumb questions. Several pups began to crowd around him begging him for his autograph. They peered up at him as they might at the tallest tree in the entire forest. Squatting down, Gabriel took a piece of birch from one of the pups, signed it with a flourish of scratches, and handed it back. He glanced over at his stepfather, who was smiling at him. His stepfather did not have to say the words; Gabriel could feel them: "I'm so very proud of you, Gabriel. You're absolutely the greatest"—

~

Heads turned as Gabriel entered the lunch room; faces lit up with surprise and awe. His uniform was clean now—pure white, except for the brilliant scarlet of his numerals, 32. Chopper scurried up to him before

Anticipation is three-quarters
the pleasure.

anybody else could and asked —no, begged— for his autograph. "What am I offered?" Gabriel said to Chopper. Chopper held up his lunch bag. "The whole thing," Chopper said, his eyes wide with desperation. "Yuk," Gabriel said. Someone burst out laughing. It was Christopher. Soon everyone was laughing. Chopper turned, tail between his legs, and crawled slowly away —

~

Gabriel bolted upright in his bed.

"That's it!"

Why hadn't he thought of it before!

Bounding to his desk, Gabriel pulled a sheet of birch from one of the side drawers and laid it out biased slightly counterclockwise. As he began to scratch on it, he pictured all the pups in the lunch room crowded around him, each one trying to outbid the other.

"Four wildberry tarts!"

"Five!"

"Nine! Nine wildberry tarts!"

He formed each letter with deliberate care:

Dear Mister McMurray:

I'm a big fan of yours. My stepdad is too. My stepdad thinks you're absolutely the greatest. I heard him say so tonight while he was watching you on TV. I've never heard my stepdad say that about anybody else.

I would really like to have your autograph. Would you please send it to me? I would keep it forever. I would never give it to anybody. I would let everybody see it, but I would never let anybody else have it, even if they offered me a hundred wildberry tarts.

I've got to go to bed now. I've got school tomorrow.

Thank you very much.

Admiringly yours,

Gabriel Maplewood

Gabriel folded the sheet of birch into threes and stared at a gold-framed photograph resting on the near corner of his desk. The photograph showed Gabriel and his real dad hanging upside down from the same limb, their arms folded across their chests. Gabriel remembered the day his mother had taken it, over three cycles ago now.

Vanity is trying to make
the maple of us look like the
mahogany of them.

Gabriel had not heard from his father since last February, when a birthday card had arrived two weeks late. It had been signed, Gabriel could tell, by his father's new wife.

Since moving away to the Valley of Fruited Vines, Gabriel's father had made less and less of an effort to stay in touch. The weeks between contacts had become months. The months—

Tears scudded down Gabriel's cheeks. He hung his head.

Gabriel slammed the gold-framed photo into the bottom drawer of his desk and, slipping into the hallway, tiptoed into his parents' room, where he got a stamp and an envelope from the desk-like thing his mother called her secretary.

Tiptoeing back into his own room, Gabriel sealed and stamped his letter and placed it on top of his astronomy book, where he would be sure not to forget it in the morning. He would deposit it in the mailnut on his way to school.

Crawling back into bed, Gabriel found himself much too excited to go to sleep, so he lay in his warm, snug bed with his eyes wide open, listening to a chorus of crickets chirping in perfect synchrony outside his window. Gabriel liked that word—synchrony. As he lay wide awake, he wondered how long it would take to receive a reply from Scurry McMurray.

"Touchdown! Quick, Martha, come and watch this on replay! Un-be-liev-able."

Gabriel prayed it wouldn't take more than a few days.

Five at the most—two days out, one there, two days back.

Maybe six.

The best cure for an
inflation of ego is a pinprick
of humility.

Four

Gabriel started checking the mailnut for a reply the very afternoon after he mailed his letter to Scurry. He didn't really expect an answer so soon, of course, but he was just too excited not to check anyway.

The first time he checked it, Gabriel felt only the slightest twinge of disappointment when he found nothing for him, because his expectations were only slight. With each passing day, however, his expectations grew, and therefore so did the level of disappointment he felt each time he checked the mailnut and found nothing for him. The initial twinge grew into a pang; the pang into a sting; the sting into a stab.

Then, on the very day that marked the end of the third week since Gabriel had mailed his letter to Scurry, something totally unexpected happened.

Gabriel was outside the school tree during recess, sitting off by himself, as he had been doing since the day after he had failed to catch Chopper's easy pass. He was sitting on a speckled, gray-and-black rock, facing away from the pawnut field, into the warming sun.

Normally at this time of the cycle, Gabriel would be peering up at armadas of puffy white clouds scudding over a deep-blue sea, or marveling at splendorous displays of autumn foliage. Today, however, he was turned inward. He was telling himself that Scurry McMurray was probably sitting at his desk at that very moment stuffing an autographed photograph into an envelope addressed to Master Gabriel Maplewood.

Scurry McMurray was just not the kind of squirrel who would ignore

One way to be beautiful
is to treat yourself as if
you were.

little requests from small admirers. Scurry McMurray was "absolutely the greatest."

Just then, Gabriel thought he heard someone calling his name from somewhere behind him. His first thought was that it was time to go in and someone was trying to tell him. Then he realized that he had only just come outside from the lunchroom and that it wouldn't be time to go in yet for another fifteen ticks or so.

He cocked one ear to the rear and heard the same voice again, this time even more distinctly. Not only was someone calling his name, but the voice calling it sounded an awfully lot like Chopper's!

No way, though, could it be Chopper calling him. Not after what had happened.

Feeling a breeze at his back, Gabriel decided that what he was actually hearing was just an uneven flow of air eddying around his furry ears. He was interpreting sounds the way some squirrels interpreted words—however they needed to at the moment.

If you too much wanted something to be true, he had learned—the hard way—was there any other way ?—you too much would be inclined to believe it so.

But then he heard his name being called again—this time by what seemed like an entire chorus!

He had to know for sure.

Turning his head slowly, eyes slightly uplifted, as if to admire the foliage to his left, Gabriel quickly shifted his eyes to look over his shoulder and caught a glimpse of what looked like someone waving at him from the pawnut field—

Someone who looked an awfully lot like Chopper!

If you too much wanted to see something, Gabriel reminded himself, you too much would be inclined to see it!

He waited a moment, then again looked over his shoulder, this time allowing his eyes to linger. It was Chopper! He was motioning for him to come to the pawnut field!

"C'mon!" he could hear Chopper call. "We need you!"

Too stunned to believe what he was seeing, Gabriel did not immediately react. Then, as if startled by the sound of a snapping twig, he jumped to all fours and scurried toward the pawnut field. Never mind,

The most precious of mettles
is courage.

Scurry! he screeched, inside his head, as he bounded; I'm not going to need your autograph after all!

Thanks anyway!

When Gabriel arrived on the pawnut field, Chopper explained that Tauntis Catscolder had had to leave for a dentist appointment and they needed someone good and fast to take his place—as a receiver!

Gabriel tried very hard not to show his excitement. He tried to be as cool and composed as he knew one of Chopper's buddies would be in the same situation. But he just couldn't help himself. Not only was he being assigned a real position on Chopper's team; he was being assigned one of the positions Chopper never gave to anyone other than one of his very best buddies. Gabriel felt like a butterfly newly emerged from the cramped quarters of a pupa, unfolding its magnificent wings in preparation for the rapture of first flight.

"Will you do it?" Chopper asked, in a pleading sort of way.

"Sure," Gabriel replied, beaming.

"Great," Chopper said, patting Gabriel on the shoulder. "Now we can beat these guys."

Chopper squatted down and his teammates, including Gabriel, formed a close circle around him. "Okay," Chopper said, "I want Chucky Cheeks and Bubba Jay to go deep, like this." Chopper drew lines in the dust to indicate where he wanted Chucky Cheeks and Bubba Jay to go. "And I want" — as Chopper glanced up at him, Gabriel felt a squeeze in his stomach so intense he thought he might vomit— "Gabriel to run out into the flats, like this." Chopper drew another line in the dirt.

Gabriel could barely breathe.

Was this really happening? Only moments earlier he had been sitting off by himself, completely alone in all the forest, and now here he was, not only playing pawnut on Chopper's team — having been asked — he was being included in the very first play!

Surely he would wake up any second now.

"Okay," Chopper said, "everybody got that?"

Gabriel nodded, trying to mimic the look of confidence he saw on the faces around him. "Okay," Chopper said to Stumpy Clearcut, the center, "on three."

Gabriel broke from the huddle with the other players and positioned himself on the right end of the line. As he waited for Chopper to begin

Every liar must possess in
memory what he lacks
in conscience.

barking out signals, a terrible thought jumped out from behind a tree in his mind—there was a chance that Chopper would actually throw the pawnut to him! After all, Chopper had assigned him a real position, and a real route!

Gabriel's legs suddenly felt like willow boughs; his stomach, as if it had been scratched into shreds. If Chopper did throw him a pass, he told himself, and he missed it, that would be it—for all time. No one would ever give him another chance.

Squirrels would point and snicker at him for the rest of his seasons.

Gabriel took a deep breath. He was blowing the tiniest little ember into a raging forest fire, he told himself, in a scolding sort of way. Chopper wasn't about to throw a pass to anyone he had zero confidence in. Chopper had only included him in the play because he didn't really have any choice. Every official pass receiver had to be assigned a route to run in each and every play, even if only to occupy a defender.

He had absolutely nothing to worry about.

"Nut one," Chopper called, "nut two, nut three" —

Gabriel sprang forward, bounced off Corky Gnawknotty, one of Bammer's big linemen, and then scurried diagonally to his right. When he neared the sideline, at about the spot Chopper had assigned to him, he abruptly stopped and turned.

Chopper was just cocking his arm to throw down field to Bubba Jay, who had beaten his defender and was scurrying toward the goal line. But instead of following through, Chopper pump-faked, looked to Gabriel—and threw!

For one terrible moment Gabriel felt exactly as he had the last time Chopper had thrown a pass to him—as if he had swallowed a whole tray full of ice cubes. But then, gluing his eyes on the softly arcing pawnut, Gabriel adjusted his position a step, and another, and then, using both arms, trapped the pawnut against his breast, just the way he'd seen Scurry McMurray do it a zillion times on television.

He did it! He caught it!

Yabba-dabba-do!

Squeezing the pawnut snugly into the crook of one arm, Gabriel was about to scurry toward the goal line when Bammer, lunging sidelong, hit him low, like a bowling stone. Gabriel hit hard ground face first, still clutching the pawnut in his arm.

Better to pick a pocket than
to betray a trust.

Right behind Bammer came the rest of Bammer's team, all screeching with laughter as they piled on top of Gabriel.

Barely able to breathe, Gabriel tried desperately to wriggle himself free, but there was far too much weight on him for him even to move. He felt his brain swell against his skull as if from repeated stings of a hornet trapped inside his head. "Get—off," he pleaded, in little more than a whisper. But no one got off. Instead, his own teammates, with Chopper leading the way, began to pile on top of him.

To a stab of horrific dread, Gabriel realized that his glasses were missing. "Get—off," he pleaded. "My glasses"—

Crunch.

The back of Gabriel's throat felt as if he had swallowed an entire hive of bees.

Tears welled.

Some are born to the wrong parents, some to the wrong circumstances; some should never have been born at all.

Finally, everyone piled off him.

"Nice catch," Chopper quipped, when the last pup had piled off Gabriel.

Everyone screeched.

"For a second there," Bammer said, "I thought you was gonna miss even that one!"

Everyone screeched again.

Stumpy Clearcut handed Gabriel what was left of his glasses; the frame was bent, one of the lenses was completely missing, the other lens was fractured. Gabriel put his glasses on anyway, as he had no other choice. Without whatever aid he could get from even a single, cracked lens, he would be as good as blind. He would have to beg someone to lead him back to the school tree.

Everyone screeched at the sight of Gabriel, dirt-smeared and disheveled, wearing a pair of broken glasses.

With several more minutes of recess left, Gabriel dragged himself to the tallest tree in the school grove and keeping to its backside climbed to the very top. Swaying on a flimsy bough, Gabriel felt his grip relax a bit, a bit more—

Beginning to lose balance, Gabriel dug his claws into the soft flesh of the bough.

He shivered.

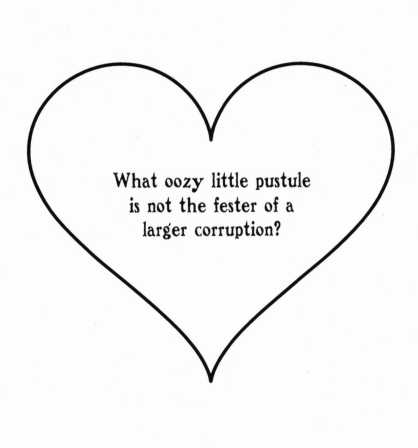

What oozy little pustule
is not the fester of a
larger corruption?

Five

As Gabriel approached the mailnut in front of his tree, Anticipation was in a dead heat with Dread. First the one would edge ahead, and then the other.

It just had to be there today, Gabriel told himself, Anticipation edging ahead.

What if it wasn't, though, Gabriel asked himself, Dread edging ahead.

Gabriel felt a rush of dizziness as he pulled several pieces of mail from the mailnut. His knees began to fail him. Afraid he might faint—more afraid, actually, that someone might see him faint and laugh at him for being such a wuss—Gabriel sat down on a speckled rock next to the post holding the mailnut.

He hadn't been sleeping well, or eating much.

He took a deep breath.

Feeling a little better, Gabriel began to sort though the mail, quickly scanning the address on each piece, even on the junk mail. He had to hold his head a certain way in order to see through the cracked lens of his glasses. Each time he failed to see his name on the first line, he felt sharp claws dig into his stomach. Coming to the last piece, he hesitated a moment, took a deep breath, and scanned the address. His heart sank. It was a letter for Cherice, from Barry Berrybury, one of the star players on Cherice's school's pawnut team. Since Cherice had been voted captain of her cheerleading squad, she had become even more popular.

Gabriel hung his head.

Why hadn't Scurry McMurray answered his letter? It just couldn't be

Logic is the father of all
possibility; possibility, the
mother of all existence.

because Scurry didn't give a care, Gabriel told himself, because Scurry McMurray wasn't like that. Scurry McMurray was different. Scurry McMurray was "absolutely the greatest." Scurry McMurray was somebody the whole forest looked up to. Scurry McMurray was a genuine, real-live hero, and genuine, real-live heroes just did not go around hurting the feelings of little pups by treating them as if they didn't even exist.

There had to be another reason.

Gabriel watched an ant pull a dead beetle five times its own size over a small twig.

Maybe Scurry hadn't had enough time yet, Gabriel said to himself. This was, after all, the absolute busiest time of the season for professional pawnut players.

But how much time did it take, really, to sign a photograph and drop it in the mail?

Hunching forward, Gabriel held his chin in his paws.

There could be only one other explanation, he finally decided. His letter had never arrived at the Forest of the Towering Pines. Either some scathead had swiped it out of the mailnut before Old Mister Grayback could pick it up or it had somehow gotten lost in transit.

The first possibility wasn't very likely, though, Gabriel decided, because it meant someone would have to have been watching his every move. Not even Chopper or Bammer would have gone to all that trouble.

So his letter must somehow have—

Old Mister Grayback!

Old Mister Grayback was really, really old, Gabriel reminded himself, and really, really old squirrels were always forgetting and misplacing things! Just like his Grandmother Shortpine, who had gotten so confused and forgetful that his mother had had to put her in a nursing grove.

Then Gabriel recalled how his stepfather was always referring to the Forest Mail Service as a 'contradiction in terms', and was always saying things like, "You can't trust anybody to do their job anymore," and "Nobody gives a scat."

So it wasn't just old Mister Grayback. It was everybody!

Fixing his eyes on the ant pulling the dead beetle, Gabriel thought about sending another letter to Scurry McMurray, but then asked himself: If no one in the entire Mail Service could be trusted to do his job,

The rarest of gems is
the listener.

how could he ever be sure anything he sent to Scurry would ever actually get to him?

Gabriel watched the ant pull the dead beetle over a dead leaf, which, in relative terms, was a veritable mountain.

He snapped upright.

"Eureka!" he screeched.

If Mulberry won't come to the mountain, then the mountain will go to Mulberry!

He would deliver his letter to Scurry McMurray himself!

In person!

Jumping to his hind paws, Gabriel felt a sense of power such as he had never felt in his entire life. "I don't really need to rely on anybody!" he screeched, flinging himself into a back flip, still wearing his pack. "I can do it all myself!"

Gabriel scurried up the tree and into his bedroom. Cherice would be home any minute, so he had to hurry. Digging his hiking pack from the floor of his closet, from under last year's Halloween costume, Gabriel quickly began filling it with things from his chest of drawers. He wasn't sure exactly what he would need, so he just grabbed a few things from each drawer.

The last thing he stuffed into his pack was his bathing suit.

Gabriel pictured himself floating on a raft in a tranquil basin at the foot of a gigantic waterfall deep, deep in the forest. A brown-eyed doe and her spotted fawn were drinking from the near shore. The doe winked at him; he winked back.

Scurrying into the bathroom, Gabriel stuffed his incisor brush into a side pocket on his backpack and was about to grab the tube of incisor paste from the medicine cabinet when he caught a glimpse of his broken glasses in the mirror. His heart sank. He couldn't go anywhere without an intact pair of glasses. If the one remaining lens were to fall out, he would never be able to find his way home again. He would be lost in the forest forever.

Then he remembered!

His mother had made him keep his old glasses for just such an emergency!

Scampering back into his bedroom, Gabriel found his old glasses in the drawer of his night stand and put them on. They were a little

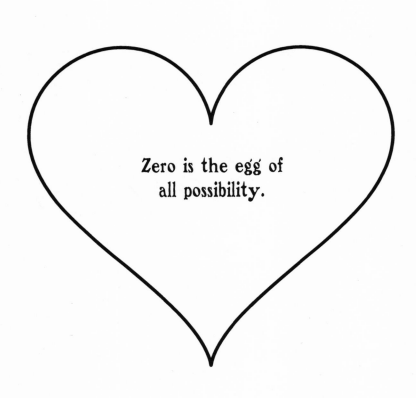

Zero is the egg of
all possibility.

blurry, but not bad. Not bad at all! Besides, the more hardships he had to overcome, the better. Scurry McMurray would be just that much more impressed with his effort, and just that much more likely to write something really nice on the photograph he would give him . . . in person!

Scurrying into the kitchen with his pack, Gabriel looked at the wall clock. Sharp claws dug into his stomach. Cherice was usually already home by now!

He couldn't leave, though, without packing something to eat; he would starve to death before he ever got to the Forest of the Towering Pines.

Using a chair from the kitchen table, Gabriel lifted the treats canister down from the shelf over the refrigerator and began stuffing chocolate-covered walnuts into his pants pockets. There were just enough left over from celebrating Cherice being elected captain of her cheerleading squad to fill both front pockets.

Hey, if ever there was in fact a 'special occasion,' for him anyway, this was it!

Strapping on his backpack, Gabriel bounded to the main holeway and peeked out to see if his sister was in sight.

She was!

She was standing near the bottom of the tree with Rhett Cinquefoil, who had been walking Cherice home from school since the day after she had been elected captain of her cheerleading squad. Rhett, who looked as if he had just stepped out of one of Cherice's celebrity magazines, lived in a grove a few furlongs down the path.

Listening to his big sister giggle in that dumb, flirty way of hers, Gabriel wished there were some way he could make Rhett aware of the letter from Barry Berrybury waiting for Cherice out in the mailnut. Hey Cherice! Gabriel pictured himself calling down to his sister. There's a letter for you from out in the mailnut—from someone named Barry Berrybury.

Pulling his head from the holeway, Gabriel scurried to his room, removed his hiking pack, and stood next to his window hole, with both ears cocked toward the opening. He listened until he could hear the sound of claws against tree bark. When he could no longer hear it, he squeezed himself through the hole, pulled his pack through, and scurried to the ground, and into the forest.

He stopped only when he was sure he was well out of Cherice's sight.

When all else fails, try
thinking for yourself.

Taking a deep breath of cool, moist air pungent with the scent of moldering leaves, Gabriel found himself filled with a whole dessert menu of delicious feelings. He felt free—freer even than in that magical moment each June when school let out for the summer. He felt independent—for the first time in his life, he was neither answerable to nor dependent on anyone. He felt adventurous—the way he imagined the great pioneer squirrels must have felt when they were forced by the saws and axes of the two-leggeds to find new places to live.

The most delicious feeling of all, though, came as Gabriel pictured his mother and stepfather staring down at his empty bed. He savored their regret, their guilt—their agony.

He took one last deep breath and began to look around for a tall tree to climb. He had never before been to the Forest of the Towering Pines, where Scurry McMurray's team, the North County Pines, was home-based, but he knew it lay to the north—which was all he needed to know.

Picking the tallest tree in sight, Gabriel scurried to the very top; determined the apogee of the sun's arc, while squinting against the bright, mid-afternoon sunlight; and descended to the ground on the opposite side of the tree. Holding his head high, Gabriel thrust out his breast, felt the reassuring bulges of chocolate-covered walnuts in his pants pockets, and set out for the Forest of the Towering Pines—the bravest, cleverest, freest pup in all the forest.

More than moolah, we
need meaning.

Six

As Gabriel ventured ever deeper into the forest, he would sometimes, on whim, scuff his paws through the freshly fallen leaves, just to hear them rustle. Now and then, on whim, he would pause to sniff the cool forest air, which he found, to his delight, to be freer of two-legged taintings than any air he had ever sniffed before in his life. Upon hearing the clear, liquid flutings of a wood thrush, he would stop to listen, and then nod in gratitude. Upon sighting an incandescent birch or a flaming maple, he would stop to marvel, and then nod in gratitude. Whenever the fancy struck him, he would pull a chocolate-covered walnut from one of his pants pockets and while nibbling at it relish the freedom to snack whenever he wanted, as often as he wanted, as much as he wanted. Every few furlongs, he would climb a tree to reassure himself he was still on course; and amidst all this, he would lapse into thinking thoughts big and small.

Gabriel could not recall having been happier in all his seasons.

But then, as the warmth and brilliance of the afternoon began to give way to evening's inevitable attenuations, the forest began to grow shadowy, the air, damp and chilly, and Gabriel began to feel less and less content with being free, unbeholden to anyone, and far deeper in the forest than he had ever been before.

Then, with a start, Gabriel realized he had entered an area in the forest in which many of the larger trees had been removed by the two-leggeds, leaving behind smaller, less healthy trees, which were too small for roosting, and too far apart for jumping from one to the other. Because of an

Before success might smile,
discipline must frown.

increased amount of sunshine reaching the forest floor, the underbrush was thicker and therefore more useful to predators.

Gabriel had not anticipated this. He had just assumed he would have his pick of large, tall roosting trees.

"You must constantly, constantly anticipate," he could hear Master Learned screech in Forest Survival class. "Which means not only looking ahead, but thinking ahead."

He had to find a safe place to roost—and soon!

It was growing dark rapidly.

Gabriel thought about turning back, but he did not know how far he would have to go to encounter the tall trees he had passed though earlier, because he had not been attentive. He had been too busy thinking thoughts big and small!

As the shadows deepened, Gabriel began to sense he was not alone, and without making a conscious decision to do so, he began to whistle through his incisors, to let whatever might be lurking in the shadows know he was just a friendly little pup, just passing through.

Crickets began to chirp—an owl hooted—Gabriel stopped whistling and began to step as soundlessly as he possibly could.

He froze!

He had heard something!

Or had he?

Using his ears like eyes, Gabriel probed the shadows in every direction for a repeat of the same sound.

He should have been listening instead of whistling, he scolded himself.

Holding his breath, Gabriel cocked his ears—and heard the sound again—

"Danger! Danger!" he could hear Master Learned screech, after playing a recording of the exact same sound. "Predator on the prowl! Predator on the prowl! Did you notice how faint it was? The fainter it is, the more dangerous it is. Can anyone tell us why?"

"Because predators are always trying to be as quiet as possible," Gabriel had replied, inside his head, unwilling to invite the scorn of his classmates by raising his paw.

Still holding his breath, Gabriel lifted himself to his full height and cocking his ears front to back heard the same sound, but from behind!

Play not to win, but for the struggle; the sweat is the victory.

Lowering himself to all fours, Gabriel crept slowly forward, as if not yet alarmed, then crept a little faster—then froze to what sounded like a snapping twig!

"Danger! Danger!" he could hear Master Learned screech. "Make one false move now and you're just another lump in some pooh-breath's stew!"

Moving not a muscle, not even to cock an ear, Gabriel probed the shadows ahead for the slightest movement and sniffed the damp air for the faintest scent.

Then he heard a different sound!—a low growl?—to his left!

And another!—a snort?—to his right!

He was surrounded!

Beginning to tremble—inside, it seemed, as well as out—Gabriel pictured himself snuggled into a tight little ball in his warm little bed. He couldn't imagine how he had ever thought it important for him to get Scurry McMurray's autograph.

Did something move?

A shadow within a shadow?

"If you sense something move," he could hear Master Learned screech. "You move! You don't wait for confirmation. You go! Now!"

Springing into the air like a grasshopper, Gabriel bounded this way and that; scurried and scampered and scurried; bounded this way and that; scurried and scampered and scurried; and seeing a grove of large tall trees dead ahead, leapt onto the trunk of the nearest tree and digging his claws into reassuring bark climbed as fast as he could, circling as he ascended. As he climbed, he heard what sounded like claws, large and sharp, digging into tree bark close behind.

His heart pounding in his breast, Gabriel climbed until he felt the bough beneath him yield. He wanted desperately to climb higher, but there was nothing to climb.

He wished he had been born a bird.

A wood thrush.

Digging his claws deeply into soft pine flesh, Gabriel probed the gloom below for the slightest indication of a presence. Only after detecting nothing for what seemed like hours—not a sound, not a hint of movement, not a scent—was Gabriel finally able to convince himself that whatever had been after him was not able to climb any higher. If it had been able, he concluded, it would surely have done so by now, there

The only true gift
is anonymous.

being no reason for it not to. What it was doing instead, Gabriel figured, was laying in wait, knowing that its quarry would ultimately yield to fatigue or hunger—or to a lack of patience. In fact, it wasn't a greater level of cunning or agility that was the primary advantage of the predator, Gabriel knew, but a greater store of patience.

Beginning to shiver, Gabriel tried to change his position so his chilled body would catch less wind, but when he loosened his grip, he came precariously close to losing his balance. His backpack, Gabriel now realized, by elevating his center of gravity, was making him less stable. All those things he had indiscriminately packed to serve as his dear friends were now acting as his worst enemies.

Interesting, Gabriel mused, through his fear, how a positive in one context could become a negative in another, just like that. Nothing is good or bad, he composed in his head, as if scratching into his journal, but that context makes it so.

Tightening his grip, Gabriel considered trying to remove his pack and letting it fall to the ground, but quickly decided against making the attempt, because loosening his grip at this point, enough to allow him to shed his pack, would likely make him even more susceptible to losing his balance.

He would stay right where he was, the way he was.

"If your tail doesn't have a kink in it," he could hear Master Learned screech, "don't put a splint on it!"

Shuddering to a chill, Gabriel was reminded of how desperately hungry he was—and then, to a rush of school's out joy, was reminded of the two pocketfuls of chocolate-covered walnuts he had thought to bring!

Woohoo! Gabriel Maplewood had anticipated! Gabriel Maplewood had thought ahead!

What a clever little squirrel Gabriel Maplewood was!

Keeping himself crouched as low as possible, to keep his center of gravity as low as possible, Gabriel freed his left paw and carefully slipped it into his left pocket to retrieve a juicy chocolate-covered walnut. To his surprise, however, his paw encountered not a morsel! All he could come up with, despite increasingly desperate probes, was a piece of walnut meat about the size of a juniper berry. Using his other paw, Gabriel frantically searched his right pocket, but all he found was a little wad of tissue.

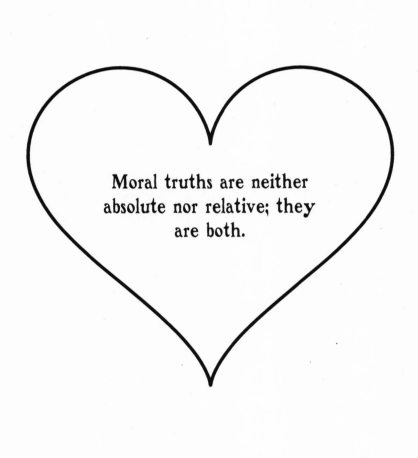

Moral truths are neither
absolute nor relative; they
are both.

Gabriel desperately searched both pockets again, but found nothing. How could this be?

Then Gabriel pictured himself snacking on chocolate-covered walnuts as he ambled through the forest without a care in the world, partaking whenever he wanted, as often as he wanted, as much as he wanted.

"You stupid scathead!" he screeched.

He had treated his pockets as snack jars that some invisible hand would keep filled no matter how many times he reached into them, just as his mother always kept the snack jars at home filled no matter how many times he and Cherice reached into them.

He had not anticipated at all! He had simply indulged himself, and now he was getting his just deserts—not to mention his just desserts.

Hanging his head, Gabriel wished perhaps the oldest of all wishes—to be able to reach back in time and retrieve a moment badly used; then, perking up a bit, he reminded himself that he had at least something to eat. "Something is always better than nothing," he could hear Master Learned bark in Winter Survival class, "whether it's three seconds left on the clock in a pawnut game or three acorns left in the pantry in mid February."

Gabriel used his left front paw to maneuver the tiny walnut morsel up to his chattering incisors. Just as he was about to take a nibble, however, his entire body convulsed to a stinging chill, causing him to lose his grip on the walnut morsel. In a fit of panic, Gabriel freed his other front paw from the pine bough he was resting on and tried to catch the precious nugget of protein and fat before it could drop out of reach. As he did, the weight of his backpack shifted abruptly and he lost his balance.

For one terrible moment Gabriel's entire being was consumed by knowledge certain that he was going to plummet directly into the jaws of some hideous, amber-eyed monster below!

Scrambling frantically, Gabriel managed to catch hold of the pine bough with just a single front claw, while maintaining a desperate grip with his hind paws. He was now hanging upside down, with his own weight and that of his pack working fully against him. He could feel a single right front claw slowly rip through the soft, sappy flesh of the pine bough.

When it ripped all the way through, he would plummet to his death! No one would ever find him.

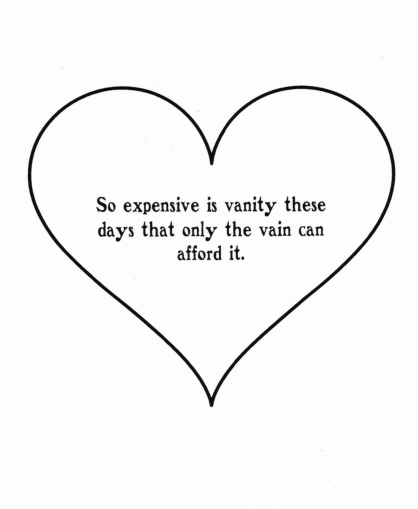

So expensive is vanity these days that only the vain can afford it.

Gabriel's brain felt like tapioca being whipped into a froth. Then he heard a voice, deep and sure, booming from the front of the classroom: "The very worst thing you can do in any life-threatening situation is to panic. Panic is fear on fire. Panic is the complete and utter absence of rational thought. Throw water on that fire! Think! Think! Think!"

Gabriel threw a bucket of water onto the fire.

A second.

A third.

Stiffening his upper body then, Gabriel pulled his torso upward and simultaneously reached for the pine bough with his left paw. He missed and felt both hind claws and the single right front claw tear through soft pine flesh. He tried again. He missed again.

About to rip free of barely any hold at all, Gabriel made one last effort, this time putting everything he had into it—and felt the claws of his left front paw dig into soft pine flesh. Pulling himself upward then, Gabriel was able to get a firm grip with all eight front claws, while simultaneously affirming the grip of all ten hind claws. Hanging like a 'possum, Gabriel rested a moment, then deftly maneuvered himself until he was right-side-up on the pine bough. Pressing himself tightly against the bough, to lower his center of gravity to the extent possible, Gabriel peered into the inky gloom that had swallowed his only morsel of food.

If only he hadn't eaten all those chocolate-covered walnuts earlier, he moaned. If only he had stopped to think. If only he had anticipated.

If only—

Half of knowing is knowing
who to ask.

Seven

Gabriel watched a pallid glow on the eastern horizon grow slowly into an ever deepening encroachment of pink and lilac, and more rapidly then into an aggressive conflagration of orange and red. As he watched, he began to wonder if what he was seeing was not a sunrise at all but actually a forest fire burning its way toward him. He wondered what it would be like to feel flames licking at his hind paws like the tongues of dragons—

It couldn't be any worse than freezing to death, he told himself, his body shuttering to another chill.

Peering up at the sky overhead, Gabriel watched the last star fade from view. He was glad to see it go. There was something about stars—their perfect aloofness maybe, or perhaps the coldness of their feeble light—that made an uncaring world seem all the more uncaring.

As the ambient gloom retreated, Gabriel began to search the trunk and limbs directly below for any sign of a menace laying in wait. He sensed nothing out of the ordinary. Finally, when the sun had risen fully above the tree line, Gabriel decided it was safe enough to begin a cautious descent.

Still shivering, he inched down the trunk head first, pausing frequently to scan for the slightest movement, to listen for the faintest sound, to sniff for the faintest scent. As he descended, he moved in a spiral, so he could search the full circumference of the tree.

When finally he reached the ground, Gabriel took only a few steps at a time away from the safety of the tree. He ventured in one direction a few steps, sat up to scan and sniff, then ventured in another direction a few

The true leader runs not for
office but from it.

steps, and did the same. When assured there was no menace nearby, he shifted his attention to the gnawing emptiness in his stomach.

Although there was not an oak tree to be seen, therefore not an acorn to be had, Gabriel reminded himself he had just spent the night in a pine tree. Pine trees produced pinecones; pinecones contained pine nuggets. And, although pine nuggets had never been one of his species' or personal favorite foods, when Gabriel thought about them now, a very strange thing happened—scaly, woody, normally unappetizing pine nuggets took on all the savory, mouth-watering appeal of juicy wildberries!

In fact, he couldn't wait to get his paws on a big, fat pine cone!

Selecting a larger tree than the one he had spent the night in, Gabriel climbed to its upper branches and quickly gnawed through the stems of several pine cones. He paused to listen to each cone fall through the feathery limbs below and hit the ground with a dull thud, which, Gabriel suspected, was not as loud as it might be if the ground were not blanketed with several cycles' accumulation of pine needles. When he was sure he had harvested enough pine nuggets to fill the emptiest stomach he had ever had in all his seasons, Gabriel scurried down the tree, picked up the nearest pine cone with both front paws, and began to devour its woody little seeds.

As he ate, Gabriel wondered, with surprise verging on bewilderment, why he had never liked pine nuggets before. Surely he had never eaten anything in his life that tasted so scrumptiously delicious.

When he could eat not one nugget more, Gabriel began to yawn and his eyes began to feel too heavy to keep open without the aid of several incisor picks. Realizing he hadn't slept all night long, he decided he'd better take a nap before he headed home.

Assuring himself he would be home to his own bed well before dark, simply by reversing his course, Gabriel climbed the pine tree he had just foraged and stretched himself out on a sturdy upper branch.

All was well.

With the sun shining warmly on his face, Gabriel stretched his arms and legs, took a deep breath, and closed his eyes—

To see our children succeed,
we need only give them
our time. To see them fail,
we need only give them
our wealth.

Eight

When Gabriel awakened, he was shivering—and completely disoriented.

Where was he? How did he get here?

Then he remembered.

Rising to his full height, Gabriel looked up at an overcast sky. Sharp claws dug into his stomach. Without the sun to guide him, he would not be able to find his way home!

Gabriel closed his eyes and drew in a deep breath, held it a moment, then let it out of its own weight. Think, he told himself. Think! Think! Think!

There had to be another way.

As Gabriel thought, he found himself staring at a peculiar-looking knot on the trunk of the tree he was in. Suddenly an idea popped into his head. If he were able to recognize trail marks—trees he had stopped to stare at, leaves he had scuffed, that sort of thing—just enough of them, he would be able to retrace his steps.

It was worth a try!

Scurrying to the ground, Gabriel circumvented the tree in which he had slept, in an ever-widening spiral, but saw not one thing familiar.

If only he had paid more attention along the way, he chided himself, hanging his head.

If only he had thought to make gnaw marks on tree trunks.

If only he had anticipated.

If only, if only, if only—

Collapsing onto a soft bed of moss, Gabriel began to weep. As he

We need to take the money
out of sports before sports
takes the money out of us.

wept, he hoped someone would hear his sobs and touch him gently on the shoulder, just like in the movies. But, of course, no one came. By the time Gabriel's sobs trailed off to a few last, halting sniffles, the moss beneath him felt damp.

Keeping his eyes closed, Gabriel curled his body up a little tighter, as if to get snugger in his warm bed at home, and told himself he was just having another bad dream. When he opened his eyes, he would actually be in his own bed. It would be Saturday morning. His sister would be on her phone in her room, talking to Sally. His stepfather would be out playing golf. His mother would be out shopping for the coming week.

He would have the whole day to himself. No, two whole days! He had almost forgotten—he didn't have to go to church anymore!

Woohoo!

Slowly raising his head from his pillow, Gabriel turned his head toward his nightstand, squeezed his eyes a little tighter, then popped them open. Instead of finding himself staring into the familiar face of his alarm clock, however, he found himself staring into the face of a wood sculpture gnawed into the shape of a heart.

You're dreaming, Gabriel told himself.

He blinked his eyes, shook his head, and stared again. The heart sculpture remained. It was attached to a large hemlock, at about eye level, just a few tail-lengths from where he was laying. Several words had been gnawed into the face of it, but he could not make them out from where he was laying.

Gabriel tried to think of a rational explanation for what he was seeing. He could think of only one. Scanning the surrounding area, he searched for any sign of someone hiding behind a tree poised to jump out at him laughing and jeering. But he saw not a hint of anyone.

Someone, or some thing, had to be nearby, though, Gabriel told himself. Otherwise, how could this heart sculpture have possibly gotten where it was?

Gabriel crept cautiously closer to the trunk of the large hemlock, sniffing the air and cocking his ears as he inched forward. When he was within a tail length of the sculpture, he stopped and slowly read the gnawed words with his old glasses.

The progression of science is mostly a history of little Davids of truth winning an occasional battle against the Goliaths of entrenched belief.

Many look for happiness at
the end of the rainbow.
Those who find it look
no further than the
rainbow itself.

He smiled. He liked the feeling these words gave him. It was a strange feeling—the kind you get when something seems familiar but you can't quite figure out why.

These were definitely friendly words, Gabriel said to himself. They were not the kind of words that the grungies were always gnawing into the walls at school.

Gabriel was surprised now to discover that the gnaw marks on the surface of the sculpture looked strikingly like those of—

He froze.

He heard something!

Lifting himself to his full height, Gabriel cocked his ears in every direction. A chill ran the length his spine as he recalled his earlier encounter.

After a moment, he heard the same sound, but did not recognize it. It wasn't like any of the sounds Master Learned had played in Forest Survival class. Gabriel listened intently for several moments more. Assured there was no known or immediate threat, he decided to play it safe anyway. "Better safe than stew," he could hear Master Learned bark.

Leaping onto the hemlock to which the heart sculpture was attached, Gabriel climbed to just above the lowest set of branches on the tree, and clinging there, on the side of the trunk facing away from the direction

Being honest is like paddling
upstream. It's a lot easier
not to and we can't take
even a moment's break
without backsliding.

of the sound, listened intently. The strange sound seemed to be coming from behind an even larger hemlock that stood just beyond the top of a small rise. From just how far behind this tree, though, Gabriel was not able to assess from where he was clinging.

Finding himself in the middle of a tug of war—Caution pulling him in one direction, Curiosity in the other—Gabriel peered around the tree trunk and studied the area between the tree he was clinging to and the large tree that stood atop the small rise. He would find out what was making the strange sound, but he would do so without taking any foolish risks.

Climbing until he could no longer see the ground, Gabriel circled toward the source of the sound and crept onto a limb that extended toward the next closest tree. When the limb began to yield to his weight, Gabriel sprang into the air and sailed across the void separating the two trees. Landing on one of the sturdier upper limbs of the adjacent tree, Gabriel crept toward the base of this limb, until he could no longer feel it yield to his weight. He paused to listen.

The strange sound was closer now, coming from below and slightly ahead.

Creeping as soundlessly as he had ever crept in his life, Gabriel made his way to almost the very end of a limb on the other side of the second tree, then, just as the limb began to yield beneath him, he leapt to the sturdiest limb within reach on a third tree, which was the large tree atop the small rise. The strange sound now seemed to be coming from almost directly below.

Gabriel tried to scan the ground around the base of the large tree, from various vantage points, but there were too many limbs and branches obstructing his view.

He had to get closer.

Gabriel took a deep breath, resisted an impulse to turn tail and flee, and began to inch head-first down the side of the tree opposite the source of the sound. As he descended, he paused often to listen. The closer he got to the ground, the drier his mouth became, and the harder his heart pounded in his breast. Reaching the sparser branches, he began to inch around the massive trunk to where he could get a quick peek below. A quick peek was all he would need, he told himself.

He froze.

Life is like riding a horse—
it's painless to the extent we
move in rhythm to it, and
the faster we go the shorter
our time in the saddle is
likely to be.

The sound had ceased!

He had been detected!

Hanging motionlessly, Gabriel listened for the slightest indication of something moving toward him. All he could detect, though, other than the happy chatter of a chickadee just above him, and the braggadocio of a blue jay three trees to his left, was a rapid thumping in his own breast. Replaying in his mind his narrow escape of the previous evening, Gabriel suddenly realized he was headed in the wrong direction! There would not be time to turn around!

Once again, he had not anticipated!

Gabriel shivered to an image of yellow fangs ripping into his flesh.

Then he heard something entirely unexpected—

"Hey, up there—not to worry."

So startled was Gabriel by this unexpected turn of events that he lost his grip and began to fall. He scratched and scrambled to regain his hold, but to no avail.

He hit the ground with a thud. "Umph."

"Oh dear," the voice said. "Sorry if I startled you. You OK?"

Momentarily dazed, Gabriel shook his head and quickly scrambled to all fours and began to search—seemingly in every direction at once—for the source of what he thought he was hearing.

"Over here," the voice said. "You all right, young fella?"

Stretching up to his full height, Gabriel cocked both ears toward the far side of the tree.

"Come on over," the voice invited.

Gabriel remained silent, wary of being lured into a trap. Creeping to the base of the large tree, he stretched tentatively forward and took a quick peek around the bump of a large muscular root, where the root flared out from the tree and entered into the ground.

He could not possibly have seen what he thought he saw!

He peeked again.

On the far side of the tree, stooped over a slab of wood, stood an old red squirrel, his face hoary with life's inexorable wintering. On his head, slightly askew, sat a crown of hearts. The slab of wood he was standing over was beginning to take the shape of a heart. Nearby was a log from which the slab had obviously been gnawed, recently.

The process of dying ends
when we stop breathing; it
begins when we stop trying.

"How's tricks?" the old red squirrel said, flashing Gabriel a wide grin, sort of punctuating this with a wink.

Gabriel was too bewildered, too incredulous, to reply. Not only was he seeing a squirrel where he had expected to find anything but a squirrel; he was seeing a red squirrel, in the fur, for the first time in his life. The only other red squirrels he had ever seen were the ones, like Scurry McMurray, he saw on television.

Finally he managed a shrug.

"Lost?" the old squirrel asked, his smile revealing a set of white-as-snow incisors. Gabriel was surprised that such an obviously ancient old squirrel could have such young-looking incisors. Old Mister Grayback, the mail squirrel, didn't have any incisors at all, and old Mister Grayback was probably four cycles younger than this old squirrel.

Gabriel nodded.

"Happens to us all," the old squirrel said.

"Are you lost, too?" Gabriel managed to ask, hoping to the contrary.

The old squirrel smiled. "Well, not at the moment, but I was once— even more lost than I expect you are at the moment." He extended a paw toward Gabriel. "Name's Tim."

Gabriel hesitated, studying the old squirrel's eyes. Seeing not a hint of what he saw in so many other eyes, he assured himself that these were not the eyes of someone who was going to hurt him. These were happy eyes, and happy eyes were not hurting eyes. He moved closer and touched the old squirrel's paw with his own. "My name's Gabriel," he said. "Gabriel Maplewood."

"Very pleased to meet you, Gabriel Maplewood," the old squirrel said.

"And I'm very pleased to meet you, Mister Tim," Gabriel said.

Mister Tim smiled. "I bet you are. No sight like a friendly face when you're lost, is there?" Mister Tim lifted his eyes and furrowed his brow. "Hmmm, maybe I can use that." He peered down at the partially-fashioned heart sculpture. "Not on this one, though. I've already got one for—darn it."

Mister Tim pressed his eyes shut and grimaced as if he were about to pass gas.

Gabriel took a step back, just in case.

Mister Tim suddenly popped his eyes open and grinned. "Got it." He shook his head. "Little rascal almost got away from me." He looked over

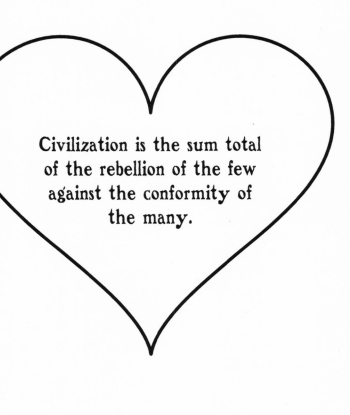

Civilization is the sum total
of the rebellion of the few
against the conformity of
the many.

at Gabriel. "'Many are called but few have the gumption to get there.' Whataya think?"

Already having a hard time keeping up with this strange old squirrel, Gabriel found himself taken aback now at being asked his opinion by an adult, particularly by one he didn't even know. Dropping his eyes, Gabriel ran the words through his mind, comparing them with their obvious counterpart in the Book of the Sacred Scratchings. He nodded. "I like it."

"Good," Mister Tim said, eyes twinkling. "It just came to me this morning. I'm trying to get it gnawed before I forget it and forget that I've forgotten it. Things tend to pop out of my head these days about as fast as frogs out of a snake pit. What'd you say your name was?"

"Gabriel. Gabriel Maplewood."

"Nice name. Pick it yourself?"

"No, my parents did."

"Well, be sure to thank them sometime. Every once in a while our parents do something right. They can't seem to help themselves in that regard."

As Gabriel stared at this strange old squirrel, the word "senile" came to mind. His mother had once used this term to describe his grandmother, who would sit and mumble all day long in a rocking chair in her nursing grove, saying mostly things that didn't make any sense.

But if this strange old squirrel were senile, Gabriel had to wonder, how could he have detected him earlier, when he was still hidden on the other side of the tree and being very, very quiet?

"How did you know I was there?" Gabriel could not wait another moment to ask.

Mister Tim smiled. "Well, young fella, when you live as deep in the forest as I do, either you learn to be aware of everything that's going on around you or you don't get to grow old and weird enough for pampered city folks to suspect you've fallen out of too many trees."

Gabriel tried to hide his guilt behind a self-conscious smile.

"Actually," Mister Tim continued, with a wink, "I heard you long before I spoke to you. You were sending me so much information I was having a hard time keeping up with it all."

"I was?"

"How's this? You jumped two trees, at a rather precarious height, to

Character is what it takes
to admit our mistakes to
ourselves; courage, what
it takes to admit them
to others.

get to this one, presumably to investigate a sound I was making no effort to conceal. This told me you were a curious sort, and courageous enough to take a significant risk to satisfy your curiosity, but prudent enough not to take too foolish a risk. Your signature on the upper limbs told me you were a young squirrel, a gray, but that, despite your youth, you had already jumped a lot of trees in your young life, often at great heights, and probably not always just for the fun of it. How'm I doin'?"

"Wow," Gabriel said. "I wish I could do that!"

"Ah, but you can," Mister Tim said. "Given the right kind experience, anyone can. The trouble is, today there's little opportunity, and even less necessity, for squirrels to get that kind of experience. Context, you see, is everything. If we live in a world of machines and gadgets, we become wise in terms of machines and gadgets. If we live in the world of nature, we become wise in terms of natural phenomena. What our world is our context is and we are."

"Nothing is good or bad but that context makes it so?" Gabriel offered, ever so tentatively.

"Oh my goodness!" Mister Tim screeched. "Yes!—yes, yes, yes."

Gabriel was surprised by Mister Tim's exuberance; even more surprised by what appeared to be tears in the old squirrel's eyes. "How long do you have to be out here before you can read sounds like that?" Gabriel asked.

Mister Tim brushed his cheeks with a paw, and smiled. "Well, a bit longer than you'd like to be, I suspect." He winked. "At least at this early season in your life."

Gabriel marveled at Mister Tim's uncanny ability to read not only Gabriel's outer sounds but his inner ones as well.

Mister Tim sat down on the log from which he had gnawed the slab of wood he was shaping into a heart. "So, now tell me, Gabriel Mapleseed," he said, straightening the crown of hearts on his head, which thereupon slipped to one side again, "what brings you so deep into the forest?" The old squirrel patted the space next to him.

Grinning to Mister Tim's mispronunciation of his name, Gabriel sat down next to Mister Tim and began to tell him the story behind his becoming lost in the forest. He told the old squirrel about the letter he had sent to Scurry McMurray, and about how he had waited three whole weeks for a reply before realizing that his letter must have become lost,

Possibility is the mother of
all hope.

and finally about deciding to go to the Forest of the Towering Pines to ask for Scurry McMurray's autograph in person.

"You must admire this Scurry fella a great deal," Mister Tim said when Gabriel had finished, "to go to such lengths to get his autograph."

Gabriel was surprised that Mister Tim didn't seem to know who Scurry McMurray was. Then he reminded himself that Mister Tim was old, and that old squirrels tended to live in the past and therefore not to know very much about what was going on in the present.

"Is he your hero?" Mister Tim asked.

Gabriel nodded. "He's absolutely the greatest."

Mister Tim looked at Gabriel with a hint of sternness in his otherwise kindly eyes. "So how come you aren't your own hero?"

What a dumb question, Gabriel thought to himself. Then he reminded himself that not only did old squirrels tend to live in the past, they also tended to say very strange things. The word "senile" popped again into Gabriel's head. Squirrels who were senile, Gabriel reminded himself, sometimes didn't seem to have a very good grip on reality—as in the sad case of his grandmother, who was always speaking as if she were still a little girl. It was as if the claws of their brain just weren't able to grip the bark anymore.

Gabriel felt a sudden surge of pity for this old squirrel. He's probably just as lost as I am, Gabriel thought to himself, only he's too senile to even know it.

"Because I'm not anything like they are," Gabriel said, consciously trying not to reveal any irritation or impatience in his voice.

"They?"

"Squirrels like Scurry McMurray." You silly.

"Oh," the old squirrel said. "So I guess you know this Scurry McMurray fella pretty well then."

"Well, I don't know him personally," Gabriel said, feeling himself losing patience. "I just know who he is, is all. Everybody does. He's the greatest pawnut player who ever lived."

Mister Tim looked at Gabriel as if about to ask him to explain why two-leggeds feed birds but shoot squirrels. "Well, now you've got me all confused. First, you tell me you can't be your own hero because you aren't anything like this Scurry McMurray fella. Then, you tell me you've never even met this fella before. Help me out here. How can anyone

There are two ways to get out
of a hole—wait for someone
to come along and figure out
the first; close your eyes and
imagine the second.

possibly know who someone is, who they really are, if they've never even met them before?"

Gabriel was sure he had never met a squirrel as out of it as this old squirrel was. He was even more out of it than his grandmother!

"I've seen him play a zillion times on television," Gabriel said. "Everybody has."

Mister Tim nodded. "OK, I think I'm getting it now." He peered at Gabriel over the top of his glasses. "What you're saying is that this Scurry McMurtry fella is your hero not because of who he is as a squirrel, but because of who he is as an athlete? Is that it?"

"He's absolutely the greatest," Gabriel said. "Even my stepfather says so."

Mister Tim got up slowly from the log and gestured with his head. "If you would be so good as to follow me, young fella, there's something down here I think you should see."

"Danger! Danger! Follow no stranger!"

Once again Gabriel found himself in the middle of a tug of war— Mister Tim's kindly eyes pulling him in one direction, Master Learned's warning in the other.

Mister Tim stopped and peered back at Gabriel, who hadn't budged. "Stay several tail-lengths behind me, if you wish," Mr. Tim said, in a sad sort of way, apparently reading Gabriel's mind yet again. "You are fleet in fact; me, only in fancy."

Gabriel stood up and began to follow along behind the old squirrel. If this strange old squirrel had not stopped by the seventh tree, Gabriel told himself, he would stop anyway. He would refuse to go another tail-length.

Well, maybe the eighth tree.

Definitely by the ninth tree.

Absolutely no further than the tenth tree.

Gabriel followed Mister Tim past the tree to which the "rainbow" heart was attached, and then past several other trees. Finally, after the twelfth tree, they came to a tall hemlock to which another heart sculpture was attached.

Mister Tim stared at the sculpture a moment, lips pursed. "I'm still not sure this one says exactly what it wants to," he said, "but if you would

The truly religious are those
who stand in silent reverence
before the ineffable mystery
of All That Is.

be so kind as to read it anyway, and let me know what you think, I'd be most appreciative."

To worship others is to
regret ourselves

Stepping forward, Gabriel pushed his old glasses closer to his eyes, for better focus, and then carefully read the words gnawed into the face of the heart scupture. He felt the back of his throat begin to burn, as if from the sting of a swallowed bee.

"You daydream about this Scurry McMurtry fellow a lot, don't you, son?" Mister Tim asked. "About being able to play pawnut like him; about getting the kind of recognition and validation he gets."

Gabriel looked up at Mister Tim in wonderment. How did he know?

Mister Tim winked and then sat down, with a grunt, on a nearby log that had been gnawed on one end, perhaps three seasons ago. He invited Gabriel to sit next to him.

Gabriel sat.

"Now, this may come as a bit of a surprise to you, my young friend," the old squirrel said, "but I was once young myself. I know, I know—it's hard to believe, but it's true. I was once even exactly the age you are now, and when I was, I didn't think I could be my own hero either. I wasn't able to see anything particularly noteworthy about myself, and no one took it upon themselves to help me. My father never really got involved in my life, and my mother, well, she did the best she could. One or two of my teachers took at least some interest in me, but, in retrospect, I can see that most of them were just trying to survive, too. So, instead of

There comes a time when
we can no longer blame
either our parents or our
circumstances for what we
are or are not.

discovering and getting comfortable with who I was as a one-of-a-kind rodent in all the Great Forest, I spent all my early seasons, and a good many of my later seasons as well, wishing I could be anything but who I was. I thought I had to be like the squirrels who were always being held up as examples of the only kind of success that mattered. But, of course, it was always a hopeless prospect. They were always athletic and glib and mostly grays, while I was nerdy and nearsighted and hopelessly red."

Mister Tim smiled at Gabriel over the top of his glasses, but there was a noticeable diminishment in his eyes, as when the sun is partially veiled by gauzy clouds.

"Anyway, it finally dawned on me," Mister Tim continued, casting his eyes toward the ground, "that the reason I was always looking to other squirrels and wishing I could be just like they were was because I didn't appreciate who I was. No one else had ever appreciated who I was, especially when I was a young pup, so I didn't have any reason to myself. When we're pups, you see, we tend to follow the lead of the adults in our lives. Where they look, we look. Likewise, where they don't look, we don't look. So, if they don't look to us and acknowledge our unique worth, we don't either. And so, instead of learning to value ourselves, we learn to value the kind of squirrels the adults in our lives look to—most of whom, unfortunately, instead of being models of the only kind of success that really matters in this world, are too often models of the very opposite."

Gabriel tried to swallow a lump in the back of his throat, but it would not budge.

"There is no one way, of course, that all of this affects each individual squirrel," Mister Tim continued. "Some of us are affected one way, some another. Some greatly, some hardly at all—or at least not as obviously. In my own case, I ended up being so lacking in self-confidence and self-esteem that I spent almost my life, up until just a few cycles ago, being unto my own self almost entirely untrue. Instead of allowing who I really was to define my life's work and the contributions I could make, I tried to be what I thought I had to be in order to be a 'proper' success. Instead of following my own voice, the one we all have, down here"— Mister Tim pointed a claw toward his red breast—"I allowed myself to be led by the tootings and flutings of various pied-pipers. I even tried to make myself be interested in things I had absolutely no interest in—as

The quality of one's waking moment is inversely proportional to the length of one's waiting commute.

a way of making myself worthy of other squirrels' attention. Of course, no matter how hard I tried to force myself to fit into these hand-me-downs, I always failed, because, of course, they weren't made for me, nor I for them. I was Timothy Peepers Tamarack, for goodness sake, not Philoneous T. Aardvark."

Gabriel smiled as a tear scudded down his furry cheek.

"Of course, the more I failed," Timothy Peepers Tamarack continued, "the worse I felt about myself. I mean, seeing yourself failing all the time—never quite measuring up, never quite being able to fit into the mold—doesn't exactly make for feeling very good about one's self, does it?"

Gabriel shook his head.

A reddish paw appeared in Gabriel's field of vision holding a handkerchief sprinkled with little hearts. "For the soul's dew," Mr. Tim said.

Gabriel used Tim's curious offering to wipe the wet from his eyes and cheeks.

"Of course, this agony could easily have gone on until the moment of my last breath," Mister Tim continued, "but fortunately it did not. Something happened, near this very spot—but, I get ahead of myself. All things in their time. For the moment, let's just say it finally dawned on me that the one squirrel I needed to be accepted by more than any other in the Great Forest was myself, and that the only way I could ever do this was simply to be myself. Instead of chasing rainbows out there"—Mister Tim pointed a claw to his right—"I needed to look for the only rainbow that really mattered, the one in here." Mr. Tim pointed to his breast, then peered up at the heart sculpture attached to the tree in front of where he and Gabriel were sitting. "Ever since then I've been gnawing these little sculptures."

Gabriel followed Mister Tim's eyes to the heart sculpture. He noticed the great care and skill with which it had been gnawed.

"But why do you keep them out here?" Gabriel asked. "Why don't you take them to where other squirrels can see them?"

Mister Tim cast his eyes downward and was silent for a moment. "Before coming out here to live," he began, "I used to live in the Forest of the Towering Pines." He smiled toward Gabriel. "Where you're bound for, I believe." He winked. "Or were bound for anyway."

Gabriel smiled.

Happiness is not a candy store of
dipped-blisses and frosted ecstasies
in some super mall in the sky,
but an eternal smile spread
over the ocean of our soul
in the moment of
our death.

"I lived there many seasons and held a variety of jobs in the inner grove, to which I had to commute every day. I loathed all those jobs, because not a single one of them involved making a real contribution. I kept moving from one to another, thinking the next one would be different, but, of course, it never was. I would go to work every morning feeling empty; I would come home every evening feeling even emptier. Gradually I lapsed into doing what most other squirrels in similar ruts ended up doing—what all those pied pipers out there keep telling us to do, in a thousand different ways—I tried to substitute superficial little pleasures for real happiness. But, of course, what good is cotton candy to a starving soul?

"The more I comforted myself with sugary little superficialities—food and drink, gizmos and gadgets, clothes and travel, that sort of thing—the emptier I felt. And the emptier I felt, the more I needed sugary little superficialities to comfort myself with. And the more sugary little superficialities I needed, the harder I had to work at meaningless jobs to get them. And the harder I had to work at meaningless jobs, the emptier I felt. And the emptier I felt, the more sugary little superficialities I needed. Around and around, down and down."

Mister Tim cleared his throat, then continued. "Of course, after a while, I had no life other than working and indulging myself, working and indulging myself, because I was too busy chasing my own tail, around and around. My family almost never saw me, and even when I was with them, I wasn't really with them, because my mind would be preoccupied with 'more important matters'. Then one day—I will never forget this moment as long as I live." Mister Tim cleared his throat again. "I was sitting in my office feeling very, well, full of myself. I had just gotten word I was up for a big promotion—the one that would finally win me 'real' success; in other words, 'real' happiness. I would even get an office with a window hole. I had just decided to leave work early to celebrate with some colleagues, when the phone rang. It was the social worker at the local hospital. My wife and my little girl pup and my little boy pup had just been massacred by a gang of two-leggeds with thundersticks."

Tim reached up and pulled the crown of hearts from his head. "My little girl, Sonia, made this for me," he explained, his voice quavering, "and gave it to me on my birthday just a week before she was mutilated."

While some of us stumble headlong
into a swamp of self-deception and
quickly drown, most of us
wander into a quicksand
of wishful thinking
and slowly sink.

Unable to speak further, Mister Tim showed Gabriel what Sonia had scratched on the inside:

For the king of my heart,

Your adoring daughter

Gabriel held Mister Tim's handkerchief toward him. Mister Tim removed his glasses, pressed the handkerchief against his entire face a moment, and then wiped his eyes.

Finally he cleared his throat.

"One day, not many seasons later," he continued, "I happened to miss my exit on my way to work—to that big job that was finally going to bring me real happiness. I had become distracted by another commuter who had been . . . rude. I was upset, not only by this other squirrel's rudeness, but by my own in return. When I realized I had missed my exit, instead of turning around, I just kept going. I opened all the windows on my fancy nutmobile, turned the radio up full blast, and, well, just sort of cast my fate to the wind—for the first time in my life.

"And this is where I ended up."

Mister Tim cocked an ear to better catch the fluty serenade of a nearby wood thrush. Gabriel cocked an ear in the same direction.

"Nice, eh?" Mister Tim said, smiling.

"It's my favorite," Gabriel said.

"Mine, too."

The two listened for a moment, then Mister Tim looked to Gabriel. "Where was I?"

"This is where you ended up," Gabriel said.

"Ah, so you were listening."

Gabriel grinned.

Mister Tim winked. "Anyway," he resumed, "at the time I left the Forest of the Towering Pines, and I can't imagine it's changed all that much since, it was filled with squirrels who weren't very happy rodents. You could see it in those two prisms we all have that parse our inner light."

Gabriel thought he heard a rumbling of distant thunder. Mister Tim didn't seem to notice.

"In trying to understand how this could be true of so many squirrels— how it could be the norm, so to speak—I came to realize that happiness, achieving it, is always a choice, a whole series of choices, actually, and that to make the right choices we have to be enlightened and willful

In the absence of coercion,
most of us lack either the
will or the discipline to
become all we are capable
of becoming.

rather than merely passive and accommodating. We have to discover what we really need in order to be happy, by asking the right questions, and then we have to act in accordance with what we discover, by finding the gumption to do it."

Mister Tim smiled toward Gabriel. "You with me?"

Gabriel nodded. He waited for Mister Tim to continue, but Mister Tim remained silent, lips pursed, eyes slightly squinted.

"Gumption," Gabriel finally said.

"Gumption," Mister Tim repeated, flashing Gabriel a grin. "Thank you. Gumption indeed. You see, discovering what we really need in order to be happy is one thing; doing something about it is . . . quite another thing. By the way, I'm distinguishing here between what we really need to be happy and what the pied pipers tell us we need." Mister Tim peered at Gabriel. "Do you know what I mean by pied pipers?"

Gabriel pictured a flute-playing fox leading a pack of smiling, carefree pups into a waiting ambush. "Things like commercials on television?" Gabriel offered.

"Exactly! Oh, you are a keen one, Master Gabriel, a keen one indeed. And real needs?—versus what the pied-pipers tell us?"

Gabriel thought for a moment. "Being with you," he said, "and seeing your sculptures, makes me feel like I've found a part of myself that's been missing for a long time but that I didn't really realize was missing until I found it. So I guess at least one thing I really need is someone like you to talk to. Is that sort of it?"

"Sort of it? That's exactly it!"

Mister Tim squinted and pursed his lips, then peered quizzically over his glasses toward Gabriel. "Was I going someplace in particular?"

Gabriel grinned. "I asked you why you didn't put your hearts up where other squirrels could see them."

"Oh yes." Mister Tim patted Gabriel on the arm. "Thank you. You are a most attentive young pup. Anyway, after abandoning the Forest of the Towering Pines and coming here, I found myself so exhilarated over having finally—well, let me ask you this. Have you ever lost something very dear to you, only to discover that you hadn't really lost it at all; it was right where it was supposed to be all along, and on realizing this you felt this chocolate-fudgy sense of relief?"

Gabriel smiled.

To understand the inherent
reluctance of men to ask for
directions, one must appreciate
the fact that not so long ago
there was no one
to ask.

"Well, that's the way I felt after finally finding, well, me. And there's something about it. When you're happy, really happy, you want everybody else to be happy too. You feel this, well, this sense of duty, I guess you could say, to do something to help bring the same kind of joy to other squirrels. I thought long and hard about what I might do in this regard— there seemed so little I could do—but then, in a flash, I pictured myself gnawing these little heart sculptures. My Sonia had planted the seed for my doing exactly this, even though, of course, I had not realized it at the time. My hope was that these sculptures might serve as little reminders of what squirrels already knew in their hearts but had forgotten because of the way we all live our lives these days.

"Once I had accumulated four score and ten of them, over several seasons, I decided to take all I could carry to the Forest of the Towering Pines and hang them up wherever I—"

Mister Tim was silent a moment, then continued. "It's hard to see now, in hindsight, how I could have been so terribly blind to my own arrogance. Those hearts that weren't smashed or mutilated were defaced with every hateful word I hope you will never in your life hear." He paused. "Instead of serving as an agent of reminding, I became the reminded—of a truth indeed I should have thought to hold above all others: Humility is the last lesson learned; the first forgot."

Gabriel rested a paw on Mister Tim's arm.

Mister Tim peered toward Gabriel over the top of his glasses. "Well, that's enough about that. Now, tell me, Gabriel Appleseed, just why was getting this Scurry McMurtry fellow's autograph so important to you anyway?"

Gabriel felt the usual impulse to avoid tossing the boomerang that too often was the personal secret given wing, but then reminded himself he was in the presence of Timothy Peepers Tamarack, not Bammer or Chopper or the Reverend Willow.

"So I could show it to the letes at school," he confessed. "So they'd stop picking on me all the time."

"Oh, dear," Mister Tim said, nodding. "I sure remember how that was."

"You do?"

"Oh, yes indeed," Mister Tim said. "And I tried to handle it pretty much the same way as you. I didn't run off to get some star athlete's autograph, but I sure did try to ingratiate myself in other ways." Mister

Women who fail with men seek
the counsel of psychotherapists.
Men who fail with women
become psychotherapists.

Tim shook his head. "You know what, though; the harder I tried, the worse they treated me."

"Yes!" Gabriel screeched. "Me too!"

"When you stop to think about it, though," Mister Tim continued, "it's not really all that strange, is it? I mean, don't we all—you and me included—gravitate away from those we perceive to be weak, and toward those we perceive to be strong?"

Gabriel nodded.

"In trying to ingratiate myself to those little peacocks, instead of making myself look strong and deserving of their respect, what I was really doing was setting myself up for exactly the opposite—getting myself rejected. And of course the more I got myself rejected, the harder I tried to ingratiate myself; and harder I tried to ingratiate myself, the more I got rejected—around and around, down and down."

Mister Tim shook his head. "Of course, I wasn't really weak at all. I just didn't realize at the time what real strength was. I mean, how strong can anyone feel, for goodness sake, who spends all his time trying to do tricks for which he is ill suited?"

Gabriel tried to swallow another lump at the back of his throat.

"The worse part, though," Mister Tim continued, "was failing to realize that I didn't need those little scatheads to like me." Mister Tim peered over his glasses toward Gabriel. "You know what a secret smile is?"

Gabriel pondered a moment. "A smile no one else can see?"

Mister Tim nodded. "That's part of it. Think of the moon. How many faces does it have?"

"Two."

"One seen, one not, correct?"

Gabriel nodded.

"Same with squirrels. We have an outer face, which everyone can see; and an inner face, which only we can see. We use our outer face to express our public joy, like this"—Mister Tim forced a ridiculous smile; Gabriel giggled—"and we use our inner face to express our private joy." Mister Tim peered at Gabriel. "Know what I'm doing right now, at this very moment, besides looking at you?"

Gabriel shook his head.

"I'm smiling." Mister Tim pointed a paw at his breast. "In here. I'm reveling in a rainbow that no one can ever take away from me, or distract

Whether a glass is half full
or half empty depends on
whether the glass is being
filled or being emptied.

me from—unless, of course, I allow them to—which, unfortunately, is exactly what I did for most of my life."

Gabriel tried to do what Mister Tim was doing, but all he could see was Mister Tim appearing to stare right through him.

"Squinty-eyed squirrels with capital letters after their name tend to call what I'm feeling at this moment self-esteem," Mister Tim continued. "I prefer not to use that term myself, because I think it's too often confused with self-confidence. Self-esteem and self-confidence are very different things. Self-confidence is what we feel when we know we can do something well, like scurry down the pawnut field, or leap from branch to branch. Self-esteem is what we feel when we take a good look at ourselves in a reflecting pool and like what we see. We don't get self-esteem by getting good grades or winning competitions. We get it by being a good citizen, a good friend, a good parent, a good colleague— indeed, a good squirrel. We get it by accepting the gifts we were given; valuing these gifts no less than those of other squirrels; and using those gifts to do good deeds for good squirrels, bad squirrels, and in-betweenie squirrels."

Gabriel thought he heard another rumble of thunder. Once again Mister Tim did not seem to notice.

"If I had been reminded of this back when I was your age," Mister Tim continued, "it sure would have saved me a whole lot of heartache."

Gabriel noticed that his backpack seemed to feel a little lighter.

"Now, secret smiles are one thing," Mister Tim continued, "empty stomachs, quite another. The one does not feed the other. You must be terribly hungry."

Gabriel realized he had not been aware of being hungry until Mister Tim suggested he might be.

Mister Tim pulled a little pouch from one of his pockets and poured several roasted acorns onto the log beside Gabriel. Gabriel tried to give some of the acorns back, suspecting Mister Tim had traveled a great distance to get them, judging from the absence of oaks in the part of the forest they were in.

"No, no, you eat them," Mister Tim insisted. "When you're in the spring of your years, you need a lot of nourishment." He winked. "Come autumn, you don't need quite so much. There's a season for getting ready

To preclude the possibility of difference is to deny the true promise of diversity.

to do your work, and a season for getting ready to leave it. We are in different seasons, you and I."

Gabriel ate—

And ate and ate.

He heard another rumble.

"Is that thunder I'm hearing?" he paused to ask.

"It is," Mister Tim answered.

"Is it coming this way?"

"Yes and no," Mister Tim replied. "There's a storm located about 20 groves to the northwest, but it's moving almost due east, meaning that most of it will miss us. We may get a brief wetting, but it won't last more than a few tail flicks."

Gabriel stared at Mister Tim in amazement. How could this old squirrel possibly know that? Then he realized he was witnessing the kind of wisdom a squirrel gets from being immersed in a particular environment.

Context is everything.

Gabriel smiled, and continued eating. When he could eat not one nibble more, Mister Tim patted him on the shoulder. "Well, my young friend, I've got to get back to my work, and I suspect you'll be wanting to go—well, just where is it you'll be wanting to go now?"

"Home!" Gabriel said, without hesitation.

Mister Tim smiled.

Gabriel noticed that the ambient light had grown dimmer in the time he and Mister Tim had been chatting, likely because of the approaching storm. "But how will I find my way?" he asked. "I'm lost. I didn't think to mark my path, and I can't follow the sun because it's covered by clouds."

Mister Tim looked sternly into Gabriel's pleading eyes. "Well, I can't find your way for you," he said, "because the sun isn't out for me any more than it is for you."

Gabriel felt sharp claws dig into his stomach.

"I can tell you this, though," Mister Tim continued. "I can tell you where you can go to find your way."

Gabriel perked up his ears.

Mister Tim pointed. "Just follow the hearts."

Looking in the direction in which Mister Tim was pointing, Gabriel noticed two parallel rows of heart sculptures marking a sort of pathway

A chore performed poorly is
little sooner a monkey off
one's back than a nettle on
one's conscience.

deeper into the forest. The individual hearts were staggered such that no two hearts directly faced each other. Gabriel could see now that the first heart sculpture he had happened upon was in line with one of the two rows of hearts, and the heart sculpture attached to the tree next to where he was sitting was in line with the other row.

"Wow," Gabriel screeched. "You gnawed all these?"

"I did," Mister Tim said, "but at no small price, as I'm sure you can imagine. I've been through thirty-seven sets of these little rascals so far, and these—which I got on sale, by the way, against my better judgment—are about shot. Never get anything important on sale, my friend."

Puzzled, Gabriel looked to Mister Tim just as Mister Tim tugged both incisors out of his mouth. Gabriel stared wide-eyed at the false incisors, then at Mister Tim's toothless grin. Bursting into laughter, Gabriel squawked so hard he fell backward from the log and began to roll on the ground.

"Everything has its price," Mister Tim added. "These things cost me 849 acorns, for goodness sake, and that was with a coupon."

Gabriel, clutching his sides, squawked all the harder. When finally he was able to catch his breath and crawl back onto the log, Mister Tim's incisors were firmly back in place.

Gabriel apologized for laughing. He had never before seen a pair of false incisors extracted from their place of purchase, he explained.

"No, no, no—that's why I took them out, so you would laugh. I haven't heard anyone laugh like that since—gosh, I can't remember the last time. The jays laugh a lot around here, of course, and I laugh out loud once in a while, but that's different. Laughter needs to be shared to really be laughter, if you know what I mean. Anyway, thanks for laughing. If there's one thing I miss out here more than anything else, that's it." Mister Tim laid a paw on Gabriel's shoulder. "Now, my friend, you'd better be off, so you can find your way before it gets any darker."

Gabriel suddenly felt torn. He yearned to get home, yet at the same time he felt a strong reluctance to leave his new friend.

Once again, though, Mister Tim seemed to be able to look right inside his head, and heart. "Now, once you've found your way," Mister Tim said, his eyes twinkling, "I expect you to come back and visit me now and then. I'll be right around here somewhere, and I'll be very interested to learn how you're doing. Will you do that?"

Summer is not over until
the last rose blooms.

Gabriel nodded.

"Good." Mister Tim got slowly up from the log, Gabriel following suit "And if you're interested," Mister Tim added, "I'll show you a thing or two about gnawing wood sculptures."

Gabriel nodded eagerly. He felt much better; but then Mister Tim did something that made him feel even better. The old squirrel wrapped his arms around Gabriel and gave him a big fat squeeze. Tears flooded into Gabriel's eyes. He wanted the old squirrel never to let go. But, of course, he did.

Mister Tim gave Gabriel a few more roasted acorns to snack on, invited him one more time to visit anytime he wished, and sent him on his way. Gabriel glanced over his shoulder a few times as he walked away. Each time he did, Mister Tim waved and Gabriel waved back.

Soon Gabriel came to a heart, on his left, that was similar in size and shape to the other two he had seen. He paused to read the message Mister Tim had gnawed into it.

Career is mine eyes on me;
contribution, mine eyes
on thee.

Gabriel recalled having heard parents wish out loud for their pups to become lawyers or doctors or athletes or the like, but he could not recall having ever heard a parent wish out loud for his or her pups to become good friends, good citizens, good mates, or anything of the like.

Gabriel recalled what had happened to the sculptures Mister Tim had hung up in the Forest of the Towering Pines. What kind of squirrel,

If a noun, spend part of
each day being a verb;
if a verb, spend part of
each day being a noun.

Gabriel wondered, would want to destroy such a gift? Then he thought about the squirrels who scratched ugly words into public trees, who defaced and abused school books, and who threw litter and trash along public pathways.

Gabriel looked toward where he had last seen Mister Tim, but the old squirrel was no longer there. Suddenly Gabriel was seized by a terrible thought. Mister Tim didn't really exist! He had made him up in another dumb daydream!

But then Gabriel heard the sound he had heard earlier, at the time he had discovered the first heart sculpture. It was the sound of false incisors scraping against raw wood. He grinned.

Hearing then another rumble of thunder, Gabriel scurried to the next heart, this one on his right. Squinting through his old glasses, he read the message Mister Tim had gnawed into it.

This one made him feel a bit uneasy.

The worst thing about lying is that we usually end up believing our own lies.

It wasn't something he wanted to think about, but it was time, he knew, for him to do just that. When he got home, he would find the courage to apologize to Cherice for all the times he had blamed her for things he had lacked the courage to take the blame for himself. Likewise, he would restore to her any credits for good deeds that he had stolen from her.

Regard every stranger you
meet as a Buddha just back
from the Bodhi tree.

If Cherice got mad at him, or laughed at him for being "such a silly geek," so be it.

He didn't really need her approval anyway.

All he really needed was his own.

Gabriel scurried on to the next heart, this one on his left.

Thou shalt not confuse height
with might, size with wise,
girth with worth.

After reading the words, he thought about how he was always trying to be someone else in his daydreams—the mightiest of the mighty—someone he could never be, not in a million zillion seasons, just as they could never be him.

What a waste! From now on, Gabriel told himself, he was going to focus on just being himself—his own hero!

Gabriel grinned as he formed a mental picture of a framed photograph of himself hanging on the wall in his bedroom. He was wearing his thick glasses and holding an astronomy book, and on a front corner of the photo was scratched: All best wishes to Gabriel Maplewood—Your Hero, G. M. He wouldn't actually do this, of course, but he liked the thought. He knew Mister Tim would like it too.

Hearing another rumble of thunder, Gabriel scurried on to the next heart, this one on his right.

Every act of violence is a
flood that could have been
prevented by constructing the
dam lower not higher.

To care is to be at the mercy
of those who do not.
To not care . . .

After reading the gnawed words, Gabriel thought about Chopper and Bammer and their buddies, and about how many squirrels there were in the forest, not just at school, but everywhere, who didn't seem to give a care about anybody but themselves, and about how many squirrels there were who seemed to take great pleasure in hurting other squirrels instead of trying to help them. Just thinking about this made Gabriel's stomach feel kind of queasy.

Then he focused on the unfinished, fill-in-the-blank part of the message.

He smiled. Having a friend like Mister Tim, he thought, was a lot like having a tall oak always just a leap and a bound away, no matter where you were.

Hearing another rumble of thunder, this one beginning like a dropped bowling ball, Gabriel checked the contents of his pack to see if he had thought to bring a rain wrap.

He hadn't.

He had thought to bring his bathing suit, though!

He scurried on to the next heart, this one on his left.

Half of freedom is being allowed
to make mistakes. The other
half is being allowed to suffer
the consequences
of those mistakes.

Having is nothing if we do not
do with what we have;
knowing is nothing if we do not
do with what we know.

After reading the words, Gabriel couldn't help but smile as he recalled the time Master Learned had taken him aside and told him he had a "real gift" for using The Three Methods (jump, jiggle, and stretch) to solve birdfeeder problems. "I've never seen anyone better," Master Learned had told Gabriel.

Gabriel's smile faded now as he recalled how he was always making himself appear to his classmates to be anything but good at solving birdfeeder problems; how he was always trying instead to be good at doing other things, like playing pawnut, or acting "cool", even though it was obvious, for all the forest to see, that he just did not have the same gifts for doing those things that he had for solving birdfeeder problems.

From now on, he told himself, with a sense of resolve so strong it seemed to make him grow half a tail taller, he was going to be who he really was. He was going to use the gifts he really had, and the knowledge he really had, no matter what!

Feeling a sense of urgency now—this emanating from something other, it seemed, than mere awareness of the rapidly approaching storm—Gabriel scurried to the next heart, this one on his right.

After reading the words, Gabriel swelled up his chest. He would remember what this heart said the next time he found himself shying away from trying something new for fear he would fall flat on his face, or that someone would make fun of him.

Defeat is that which precedes self-confidence; failure, that which precedes self-pity.

Better to begin badly
than not at all.

And when he did fall flat on his face—as surely he would—many times over—from now on, instead of berating himself for being stupid or inept—instead of just giving up and going off someplace to sulk and feel sorry for himself—he would pick himself up and try again. And again.

And if Chopper and Bammer and their buddies ridiculed him, and laughed at him, he would just tune them out. He would turn his eyes inward and gaze upon the rainbow within that Mister Tim had told him about—the one that no one could ever diminish or take away from him.

Sensing a sweetness in the stiffening breeze, Gabriel picked up his pace. The rows of alternating hearts seemed endless, but Gabriel continued to pause long enough at each heart to read and ponder the inscription each one bore. Then he came to a heart that made him forget about any threat of an approaching storm.

Evil springs not from giving
the devil a willing ear—
but from allowing fear
our life to steer.

Leadership not reluctant
is not.

Gabriel read the verse on this heart several times over, feeling a little sadder each time. Tears began to roll down his furry cheeks as he recalled how the Reverend Willow had scolded him in front of the entire congregation for being a servant of the evil drat.

"Continue down this path and you shall find yourself forever treed in the Forest of Eternal Fire," the Reverend had told him.

Gabriel realized now that by asking the particular question he had, he had not so much offended the Reverend's sense of rectitude as he had threatened the Reverend's most deeply held beliefs—beliefs based far more on fear than on earnest inquiry.

If the Great Rodent didn't wish for squirrels to think and ask questions, Gabriel wished he had said to the Reverend Willow, why did he give them the ability to do just that? Just to tempt and torment them?

Gabriel decided he would ask the Reverend Willow this very question.

In private, of course.

Wiping his eyes, Gabriel moved on to the next heart and reading the words gnawed into it thought of Hoyt's Pond and the hordes of jetbees that buzzed over its once-tranquil surface dawn till dusk, all summer long. It had been a long time now since Gabriel had spent a quiet afternoon there, in his favorite spot, thinking thoughts big and small, while dangling his hind paws in the cool, clear water.

We create clamor and commotion
in our lives to the extent we
fear what might otherwise
fill the void.

Only in rising above our anger can we forgive; only in forgiving can we rise above our anger.

Reading the words again, Gabriel thought about what Mister Tim had told him about the frenzied pace of life in the Forest of the Towering Pines. He thought also about how much the adult squirrels he knew, including his own parents, seemed swept up in the same kind of frenzy. Never once had he seen either one of his parents, or anybody else's, just sitting and reflecting—perhaps on what all the clamor and commotion was really all about.

Silence seemed to be regarded as something, like cold air in February, or the evil drat, that needed to be kept at bay no matter what.

If he were to be granted just one wish, Gabriel mused, it would be that his mother and stepfather would create a sort of Hoyt's Pond—the way Hoyt's Pond used to be—at the center of their life together—or, better, a sort of eddy in the stream.

The next heart Gabriel came to made him grin just reading it.

When all else fails,
try laughing.

He remembered how good he had felt laughing over Mister Tim's false incisors. He had ended up exhausted but in a nice sort of way— lighter, freer, happier, versus the way he felt approaching the bus stop each morning. He recalled also what Mister Tim had said about laughter—that it was the one thing he missed more than anything else in being alone deep in the forest.

How very much, Gabriel thought, he would love to see his stepfather laugh—to hear him tell jokes every night at the dinner table instead of complaining about how stupid everybody at the nut factory was, or how

What wings are to the butterfly, imagination is to the soul.

corrupt all the politicians were, or how incompetent all the professional pawnut coaches were.

When he got home, Gabriel decided, he would try something. He would start telling funny stories at the dinner table himself. Not jokes, though, because he couldn't tell a joke to save his fur. He was always forgetting half the lines, including the punch line. He would tell real stories, about real things, funny things, that had actually happened to him. Maybe, just maybe, this would encourage his stepfather to start telling funny stories himself. It would be worth a try.

Still deep in thought, Gabriel turned and started toward the next heart, keeping his head down against a surging breeze. He had taken only a few bounds when he smacked head first against something very hard. Staggering backward, Gabriel found himself staring at the widest tree trunk he had ever seen in all his seasons. "Wow!" he barked, quickly forgetting about his bruised head. Lifting his eyes, he looked up and up and up until his head was stretched as far back as it would go and his mouth was hanging open as far as it would go.

Suddenly Gabriel realized why he was where he was—and what he had to do. Dizzied by the thought, he lowered his gaze and focused his eyes on a blue-gray smudge of lichen attached to the bark directly in front of him. The dizziness soon began to subside. He would be all right, he told himself, if he just didn't look up again. Then he heard, coming from above, what sounded like a mountain stream urgently carrying snow-melt to the sea.

He felt a drop of water strike the top of his head, and another strike one shoulder. Moments later he was soaked through to his skin, as if from a collapsed umbrella. Shivering, he felt an urge to take refuge with Mister Tim, but then a rumble of thunder, sounding more like a yawn than a growl, assured him that his discomfort was only temporary. Mister Tim had been exactly correct. The main part of the storm had already passed by, to the north.

The deluge would soon be over.

Continuing to look at the massive tree trunk, Gabriel took a deep breath, then counted out loud, "One, two, three—Go!"

And up he went.

And up and up and up.

And up still further, and further, and further, until, finally, Gabriel

We embrace truth not so
much with our reason as
with our courage.

reached a yielding bough at the very top of what had to be the very tallest tree in all the Great Forest. Clinging close to the gently swaying bough, Gabriel waited for the rain to cease. When only a few tardy drops were yet falling from a rapidly brightening sky, Gabriel raised his head cautiously above a tuft of stubby fir needles and found himself looking out over what appeared to be the whole world laying magnificently before him, in one grand panorama. "Wow," he uttered, in a quiet sort of way.

Never before in all his seasons had Gabriel seen anything so breathtakingly beautiful. The forest below and beyond was a vast ocean of texture and color—firs of varying verdance intermingled with deciduous trees resplendent in their autumn finery. As Gabriel gazed transfixed, the sun burst forth to the southwest and the whole forest seemed suddenly to illuminate from a source deep within itself. To the northeast, a rainbow grew to dazzling intensity against a backdrop of the receding storm clouds. Barely able to breathe, Gabriel found himself listening anew to Mister Tim's gentle reminder: Many look for happiness at the end of the rainbow. Those who find it look no further than the rainbow itself.

"Wow," he repeated.

Tears welled as a sense of well-being swelled within Gabriel's breast to an intensity he had never before experienced in all his seasons. You are all the colors of the rainbow, Gabriel Maplewood, he could hear a voice whisper, deep within, and all the colors of the rainbow are you.

Gabriel knew he would not need to scratch these words into his journal, as he would never, ever forget them.

Closing his eyes now, Gabriel drew in a deep breath and found himself thrilling in his ability to do such a thing—thrilling in his ability to thrill.

He grinned. Wow! What a piece of work I am!

It came to him then why Mister Tim had "gone on too long," and why he had only pretended not to notice the approaching storm, and why he had sent Gabriel on his way precisely when he had. Tears welled. Such a gift he had never before received in all his seasons, not on any birthday, not on any Christmas, not ever.

Squinting toward the sun, Gabriel traced the sun's arc to its apogee. He did not wish to leave, but knew he had to. It was time. He knew his way now, but Knowing is nothing if you do not do with what you

We fear death to the
extent we realize we have
not yet lived.

know. Besides, he could always climb the highest tree again, wherever he needed to, even when he was at school. All he had to do was just close his eyes and climb it, in his imagination. Not only was there a rainbow within, so too was there a highest tree!

When Gabriel reached the ground, he headed straight for home— and couldn't wait to get there, so he could imitate, to his stepfather, how Mister Tim looked without his incisors.

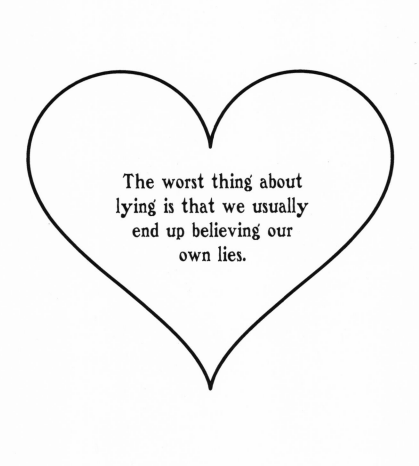

The worst thing about
lying is that we usually
end up believing our
own lies.

Nine

When Gabriel arrived home, it was past suppertime but not yet dark. His mother saw him first. As she let out a screech, a look of deep sadness vanished from her face as if by wave of a magic wand. Rushing to him, she swept him into her arms and hugged him so tightly Gabriel could feel her heart beating in her breast. Then she hugged him again. When finally she released him, Gabriel's stepfather began to scold him, glaring at him with that look Gabriel had come to know all too well. But then his stepfather's eyes softened, ever so slightly—just enough. As Gabriel moved tentatively forward, tears in his eyes, his stepfather parted his arms and the two clenched each other. It was an awkward embrace, a bit stiff, but it was a start.

When his stepfather released him, Gabriel found his sister staring at him from across the kitchen, paws on hips. "Boy, that sure was a dumb thing to do," she screeched, then she burst into tears and rushed into her brother's arms. "Don't you ever do that again, you scathead," she sniffled.

Gabriel apologized for having caused his family to worry about him. Then, wiping away his tears, he began to tell them about everything that had happened to him. First, he told them about why he had left home. Then he told them about his encounter with the unseen menace, which, he now realized, he had probably imagined, out of fear. Then he told them about spending the long, cold night at the very top of a pine tree, and finding himself lost the next morning. Then, between mouthfuls of butternut mash, which his mother insisted he eat three helpings of, he

Our behavior depends on what we value; what we value, on what we hold to be our purpose.

told them all about Mister Tim and his heart sculptures—and his false incisors.

Finally Gabriel told them about climbing the highest tree and about what he had seen from the top, and what he had realized about himself—that he was all the colors of the rainbow. When he had finished—and had eaten the last spoonful of his third helping of butternut mash—Gabriel began to yawn and to rub his eyes.

"To bed," his mother said. "You must be exhausted."

"I guess maybe I am," Gabriel said, barely able to keep his eyes open.

Gabriel gave everyone another hug, then dragged himself off to bed. Never in all his life had his little bed felt so warm and cozy.

Just before drifting off to sleep, Gabriel thought about Mister Tim. He wondered if Mister Tim's false incisors were at that very moment soaking in a tumbler of water next to his bed.

His last thought was of his stepfather smiling.

~

The next morning, Gabriel bolted out of bed at the first sound of his mother's voice. "I'm up!" he screeched. Bounding to the window hole, Gabriel drew in a deep breath of dewy air; marveled at his ability to do that on command (command to whom? What?); and watched a gold-and-crimson maple leaf, brilliant in the bright, early-morning sunlight, float languidly to the ground, joining countless cousins in covering the earth in a great patchwork quilt. He smiled to a gaggle of jays demanding each other's attention, then, whistling a made-up tune through his incisors, began to get dressed for school.

As he was tying his sneakers, he heard a rap at the door. He stopped whistling. "Come in," he said, in a restrained sort of voice.

Gabriel's stepfather peeked his head around the edge of the door. "I thought I heard a strange sound in here," he said.

"I was whistling," Gabriel confessed.

Gabriel's stepfather smiled. "I didn't know you could whistle."

"Neither did I."

His stepfather smiled, then withdrew, leaving, Gabriel noticed, the door partially open.

Resuming his whistling, Gabriel finished tying his sneakers, then looked at himself in the mirror over his dresser. He loved seeing his

If we listen only to those
voices we wish to hear,
soon there will be
no others.

stepfather smile, but he loved seeing himself smile even more! He winked, simultaneously winking back at himself, then scurried downstairs to the kitchen, where he ate three bowls of acorn flakes in record time. After clearing his dishes to the wash counter, he quickly brushed his incisors, grabbed his books, hugged everyone, including his stepfather, and scurried out the main holeway and down the tree.

Normally Gabriel would have tried to time his arrival at the bus stop with the arrival of the bus, but this morning he made no such effort.

Gabriel noticed Bammer whisper something to Chopper, who looked Gabriel's way.

"Well, look who's here," Chopper said, in that elevated voice he would always use to command the attention of everyone around him. "If it ain't the little mole who ran away 'cause he just couldn't take it—aaaawww."

Everyone at the bus stop laughed.

Bammer whispered something in Chopper's ear. Chopper approached Gabriel.

"What's the matter?" Chopper said, "Get scared of the boogey rodent and come running home to mama, did ya?"

Everyone laughed again.

Gabriel could hear them, but as if from a great distance, for he was already far, far away, climbing higher and higher.

Just then, Chopper gave Gabriel a sharp push and Gabriel fell backwards over Bammer, who had sneaked around behind Gabriel and crouched down next to Gabriel's hind legs.

Laying on his back, Gabriel peeked his head above a tuft of fir needles and gazed upon a magnificent rainbow, brilliant against a bank of receding storm clouds. He saw not the pigeon-twit, the klutz, the geek, that Bammer and Chopper wanted him to see, but an earnest, caring little squirrel who had the courage to climb the highest tree; not to mention the courage to be his real self. Gabriel saw a squirrel who could make his stepfather smile simply by making an effort to do so.

As Gabriel picked himself off the ground, he realized he was smiling. Not outwardly, such that Chopper and the others could notice, but inwardly, secretly—toward an image, as if in a reflection pool, smiling back at him.

He smiled all the harder.

The bus approached as Gabriel was brushing himself off.

Each of us has not a soul,
but soul; just as each of us
has not a purpose,
but purpose.

Looking northward, Gabriel decided he would visit Mister Tim again very soon, and when he did, he would take along a whole backpack full of acorns to put toward Mister Tim's next pair of incisors.

Gabriel grinned. He chuckled out loud.

When all else fails, try laughing!

By the time he got on the bus, Gabriel was howling.

Stumpy Clearcut was the first to start howling with him. By the time the bus arrived at the school tree, everyone on the bus, save Bammer and Chopper, was howling so hard the bus driver had to put on a pair of ear muffs.

No one had the least idea why everyone was laughing, nor cared.

Maturity is choosing the
smallest or the least when
no one is looking.

Ten

Gabriel visited Mister Tim that very next weekend, and on many a weekend thereafter. On each occasion, he brought along with him all the acorns he could carry, so that Mister Tim would never-ever have to worry about where his next pair of incisors was coming from. At first, Gabriel would watch Mister Tim work on his sculptures while the two squirrels jabbered away on all manner of topics big and small. But then Gabriel began to volunteer to do little chores, such as helping Mister Tim find suitable trees from which to harvest slabs for more sculptures. As the seasons passed, Mister Tim invited Gabriel to do more and more of the tasks involved in making sculptures, until finally Gabriel was helping Mister Tim gnaw the sculptures themselves. Gabriel made many mistakes during his time of learning, sometimes ruining whole sculptures, but Mister Tim never once scolded him. Instead, he used every mistake Gabriel made as an opportunity to teach Gabriel a new technique or skill, or a tidbit of wisdom.

One afternoon, while on his way home from a visit, Gabriel found himself smiling. He realized he was no longer afraid of being ridiculed for making mistakes.

He was free!

On the occasion of his most-recent visit, after he and Mister Tim had finished a robust lunch of roasted acorns and one whole wildberry tart each, Gabriel slipped his journal from his backpack and, holding it closed, looked to Mister Tim. "May I read something to you?" he asked.

"Is there a Jill as well as a Jack?" Mister Tim replied.

Happiness is a side effect.
Meaning is the mission.

Gabriel opened his journal, but then found himself stalled on Mister Tim's reply, which increasingly seemed less a truism in service to confirming a truth than a conundrum to be pondered until such time it might be resolved. Gabriel showed Mister Tim a quizzical look.

Mister Tim grinned. "We'll assume to the affirmative"

Gabriel cleared his throat and began to read, his voice starting out a bit unsteady but gaining firmness rapidly: In order for the Great Rodent to be all-powerful, he would seem to need to be able to create something even more powerful than himself. If he could not do this, then how could he be all-powerful? There would be at least one thing he could not do. However, if he <u>could</u> create something even more powerful than himself, and did, then he would no longer be all-powerful. What he created would be. Help!

Mister Tim smiled. "What is the sum of one plus one?"

"Two."

Mister Tim winked. "Very good."

Gabriel grinned.

"Was there ever a beginning to one plus one summing to two?"

Gabriel held pensive a moment, then shook his head. "No, there couldn't be."

"Will there ever be an end?"

"No."

"Could one plus one ever be made to sum to three?"

Gabriel smiled. "No."

"What's the opposite of plus-one?"

"Minus-one."

"Can we have the one, so to say, without the other?"

"No."

"Why not?"

"Because."

"Because the one creates the other?—makes the other necessary?"

"Yes."

"Was there a beginning to this mutual creation?"

"No."

"What do plus-one and minus-one sum to?"

"Zero."

Happiness derives not from
what we possess, attain, or
consume, but from who we
are in belief, attitude,
and behavior.

"Might we say then that plus-one and minus-one are simultaneously plus-one and minus-one and zero?"

"It would seem so."

"In other words, plus-one and minus-one at any given moment both exist and do not exist?"

Gabriel smiled, nodding.

"What about left-right, up-down, light-dark, hot-cold, near-far, and so on—where the one part creates the other part; do all such pairs essentially sum to zero?"

Gabriel saw in a flash where Mister Tim was leading him. He grinned.

"By way of extrapolation then, might we view all of reality as being simultaneously everything and nothing, existing and not existing, with no beginning and no ending?"

Gabriel nodded. "Yes."

"Are you ready to go back to work?"

Gabriel slipped his journal back into his pack. "I am."

Meaning is the ember;
fulfillment, the glow.

Epilogue

As the seasons passed, Gabriel matured into a young buck and a skilled sculptor in his own right, while Mister Tim grew hoarier, more stooped, and ever more forgetful. Mister Tim did not, however, even once, run out of incisors. In the spring of Gabriel's last year in school, Mister Tim and Gabriel climbed the highest tree one warm Sunday morning, as they customarily did to begin each new day, and gazed upon the Great Forest in solemn silence, as if they were in church. Instead of returning to their work afterward, however, they went to where they had first sat and talked together. Mister Tim invited Gabriel to sit next to him, just as he had on that earlier occasion. He spoke very quietly. "There are two ways to view this world," he said. "We can view it in terms of particles, with each particle being distinct from all others, or we can view it in terms of waves, with each wave being indistinct from all others. The particle view accommodates simplicity and certainty; the wave view, complexity and ambiguity.

"Take morality, for example. We can view morality in terms of particles, as in the case of the Two Score and Twelve Indelible Don'ts, where each Indelible Don't is a distinct rule or law. Or we can view morality in terms of waves, that is, as an infinite number of moral conundrums, with each conundrum emanating from a unique set of circumstances. The particle view might say: 'Ye shall not dishonor thy father or thy mother,' while the wave view might say, 'In the absence of a specific context—that is, a particular set of circumstances—the meaning of 'dishonor' is too vague, too open-ended, to be useful.

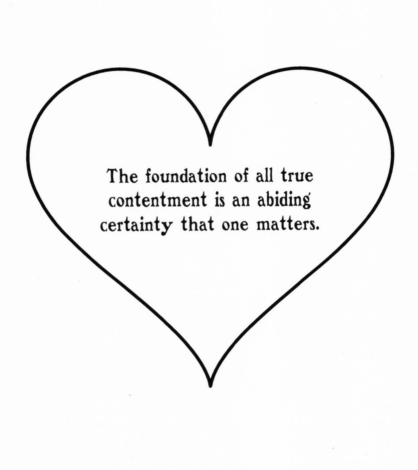

The foundation of all true
contentment is an abiding
certainty that one matters.

"There is, of course, a third way to view morality, one that does not so much represent a compromise between the particle and wave views as it does a synthesis of these. This view recognizes that there are moral principles but also that these principles cannot be articulated as absolutes; in fact, in most instances, it would, take an infinite number of words to do so. For example, regarding the rule 'Ye shall not kill,' in order for this rule to be useful, it would need to be expanded upon to address every possible situation involving the ending of a life, sentient or no. A single, simple declaration, such as 'Ye shall not kill,' would be far too general, far too lacking in specificity, to be useful in making moral judgments. In fact, if we were to embrace this particular rule as is, that is, as a moral absolute in and of itself, we would soon starve to death."

Mister Tim paused a moment, as if to gather strength, then continued:

"What we experience as morality—that is, as moral conundrums— was made necessary by an evolving brain that, once it had attained a certain level of complexity, had to begin to mediate between reflex, or instinct, and cognition. In order for it to be able to do this, however, it had to be able to bypass or modulate the absolutes that had been hard-wired into it during the early stages of its development. In other words, life had to become moral—that is, messy. If this were not the case, there would be no free will, no moral responsibility, and no benefit to be gained from having a big brain.

"Unfortunately, though, nothing comes to us in the absence of a commensurate cost. In the present case, this cost constitutes the relative ease with which our brains—our conscious minds—can be compromised or corrupted by all manner of pied piers."

Mister Tim patted Gabriel on the knee. "In your case, though, my good friend—not to worry. One can possess in this world no greater defense against the ill-intentions of rascals and ruffians than a stout heart and a wise soul."

Mister Tim patted Gabriel on the arm. "And now, my friend, it is time for you to be on your way. I have grown weary and must now lay down for a long rest."

Gabriel did as he was told, of course, but felt very uneasy all the way home. He did not sleep all that night. In the morning, instead of going to school, he scurried back into the deep forest and searched for Mister Tim. He searched everywhere, even up the highest tree. Finally

Some poems are written;
others are lived.

he came upon a freshly gnawed heart sculpture lying on the ground near the log on which he and Mister Tim had first and last sat together. On top of the heart sculpture sat Mister Tim's crown of hearts. Lifting his daughter's handiwork, Gabriel found a set of well-worn incisors, and a freshly gnawed verse.

Sinking to his knees, Gabriel rested his forehead on the heart sculpture and wept. He wept until the raw wood beneath his furry face was darkened with tears. When finally he lifted his head, he noticed a circle of acorns neatly arranged around the heart sculpture.

Gabriel smiled. He knew what he had to do. He was ready. Mister Tim had taught him well. Lifting the crown of hearts, Gabriel rested it on his head, slightly askew, and set to work.

And so it was that Gabriel Maplewood took up residence in the deep forest and set about his life's work. Many a season has since passed, and Gabriel has gone through many a set of incisors. He has grown a little hoary, a little stooped, and a wee bit forgetful, but he is still out there, gnawing away.

Acknowledgments

My editor of 51 years, Laurie E. Sandeman, insisted on reading every word of this manuscript. As usual, she found several errors and made several useful comments and suggestions. She did this despite being afflicted with Alzheimer's disease and daily migraine headaches.

About the Author

Tom Fitzgerald led a Huckleberry Finn childhood along the St. Lawrence River before undertaking formal studies in physics, mathematics, law, industrial management, and English. Tom is the author of *Poor Richards Lament: A most timely tale*. According to Michael Zuckerman, Professor of History at the University of Pennsylvania, *Poor Richard's Lament* "joins John Barth's *Sot-Weed Factor* as the best historical fiction of early America ever written."

Coming Soon
from Kingsley Books . . .

Common Sense 2.0

"Stupendous! Just stupendous! Perhaps the most exhilarating feat of political imagination of our time!" —Michael Zuckerman, University of Pennsylvania

What right did Mr. Lincoln have to prevent the South from breaking away from the Union in 1861? Was it the same right George III had to prevent the American colonies from breaking away from the British Empire in 1776?

Consider in this regard the deep divides that exist today between roughly the same demographics of 150 years ago over such issues as global climate change, abortion, school prayer, immigration, creationism, big government, political compromise, Keynesian economics, social safety nets, environmental degradation, fracking, minimum wage, regulation, gay marriage, euthanasia, trickle-down economics, gun control, Common Core, and American Exceptionalism, to name some of the more obvious issues.

Might these deep divides in fact represent irreconcilable differences? Might it be time to say good-bye: the Blue States to the Red States; the Red States to the Blue States?

Common Sense 2.0 offers the Blue States (and the Red States) a roadmap to a mutual, no-contest separation. The Blue States would finally get sensible gun regulation, universal healthcare, humane law enforcement, et al, while the Red States would finally get creationism, school prayer, deregulation, et al. Never again would the one side live in fear of being dominated by the other.

Poor Richard's Lament (two-volume set)

What if Ben Franklin had to come back?

What if everything depended on it?

Benjamin Franklin has been confined to a private apartment in the Plantation of the Unrepentant for the past two-plus centuries. Instead of contemplating his 'errata', however, Ben has added 12 more volumes to his Autobiography.

Toward forcing the issue, Ben is brought before a panel of examiners one of whom, disconcertingly, is the man who was largely responsible for Ben's undeserved womanizer rap: John Adams.

By the end of Ben's examination, in which the 'sins of the Patre Patriae' are brought devastatingly to fore, Ben fully expects to be cast into the abyss. Instead, he's invited to bear witness to what's become of America in the two-plus centuries of his absence.

Ben's odyssey of witness begins at his birth site in Boston, passes through New York (where Ben upstages a conference at the Waldorf Astoria), and ends, with wrenching poignancy, at his gravesite in Philadelphia.

Interwoven into the main story is a second, this one beginning in the red-carpeted parlors of the West Wing and ending in the bloodstained streets of West Philadelphia. Eventually, the paralleling stories collide, like massive tectonic plates, in a stunning series of shocks and aftershocks.

Following in the traditions of Dickens' *A Christmas Carol*, Capra's *It's a Wonderful Life*, and Dante's *Divine Comedy*, *Poor Richard's Lament*, eight years in the making, is an intricately woven, ultimately uplifting tale of hope and redemption, written in close consonance with the avuncular and aphoristic persona of Benjamin Franklin, Printer.

"*A grand and gorgeous book!*"—Michael Zuckerman, University of Pennsylvania.

For more information about these books, visit www.kingsley-books.com.
To order the single-volume edition of Poor Richard's Lament,
visit www.hobblebush.com.

Other Fare

In addition to a lineup of unique hardcover offerings, Kingsley Books offers several lines of one-of-a-kind greeting cards:

*A single rose is an expression of love;
a dozen,
an admission of guilt.*

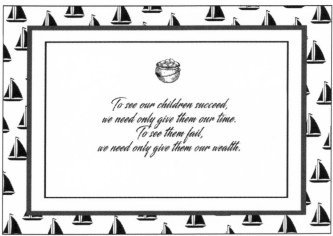

*To see our children succeed,
we need only give them our time.
To see them fail,
we need only give them our wealth.*

For details, visit:
www.kingsley-books.com

Share Your Wisdom! Publish It!

Ben Franklin, arguably one of the wisest men of his time, shared his wisdom, accumulated over eight decades, by a variety of means, including his famous Almanacks. Following in Ben's footsteps, Kingsley Books is publishing similar volumes, toward similar ends, but with a twist. KB's "wiki" almanacks are composed entirely of material contributed by men and women unaffiliated with Kingsley Books.

Poor Richard, 2020.

AN

Almanack

For the Year of Chrift

2020,

Being the Firft after LEAP YEAR:

And makes fince the Creation	Years
By the Account of the Eastern *Greeks*	7141
By the Latin Church, when ☉ ent. ♈	6932
By the Computation of *W. W.*	5742
By the *Roman* Chronology	5682
By the *Jewish* Rabbies	5494

Wherein is contained

The Lunations, Eclipfes, Judgment of the Weather, Spring Tides, Planets Motions & mutual Afpects, Sun and Moon's Rifing and Setting, Length of Days, Time of High Water, Fairs, Courts, and obfervable Days.

Fitted to the Latitude of Forty Degrees, and a Meridian of Five Hours Weft from *London*, but may without fenfible Error, ferve all the adjacent Places, even from *Newfoundland* to *South-Carolina.*

By *RICHARD SAUNDERS*, Philom.

PHILADELPHIA:
Printed and fold by *B. FRANKLIN*, at the New Printing-Office near the Market.

To learn more, or to submit an entry, visit:
www.kingsley-books.com